A second chance.

I unscrewed the gas-tank cap and dumped in the sugar, then screwed the cap on again and scurried back around the car and out of the yard.

I had done it! And no one saw me. I was safe now, as long as I could get back inside the house and upstairs without waking Mom or Dad.

I had fixed it so I wouldn't die tomorrow. Sugar in the gas tank is lousy for the engine; the car can't be driven until it's repaired. Even if I got upset again and ran out into the street, the Hazeltons' car wouldn't—couldn't—be there to run over me. It hadn't been that difficult at all.

So why had the voice said that other people failed to fix their lives?

<<REWIND

william sleator

puffin books

PUFFIN BOOKS << Published by the Penguin Group << Penguin Putnam Books for Young Readers, 345 Hudson Street, New York, New York 10014, U.S.A. << Penguin Books Ltd., 27 Wrights Lane, London W8 5TZ, England << Penguin Books Australia Ltd., Ringwood, Victoria, Australia << Penguin Books Canada Ltd., 10 Alcorn Avenue, Toronto, Ontario, Canada M4V 3B2 << Penguin Books (N.Z.) Ltd., 182-190 Wairau Road, Auckland 10, New Zealand << Penguin Books Ltd., Registered Offices: Harmondsworth, Middlesex, England

<< First published in the United States of America by Dutton Children's Books, a division of Penguin Putnam Books for Young Readers, 1999 << Published by Puffin Books, a division of Penguin Putnam Books for Young Readers, 2001 << 10 9 8 7 6 5 4 3 2

<< Copyright © William Sleator, 1999 << All rights reserved. << THE LIBRARY OF CONGRESS HAS CATALOGED THE PUTNAM EDITION AS FOLLOWS: << Sleator, William. << Rewind / William Sleator.—1st ed.   p.   cm. << Summary: Not long after learning that he was adopted, eleven-year-old Peter is hit by a car and then given several chances to alter events that could lead to his death. << ISBN 0-525-46130-2 (hc) [1. Near-death experiences—Fiction. 2. Adoption—Fiction. 3. Parent and Child—Fiction. 4. Self-perception—Fiction.] I. Title. << PZ7.S6313Re 1999 [Fic]—dc21 99-12260 CIP AC << Puffin Books ISBN 0-14-131101-0 << Printed in the United States of America

this book is for **paul rhode**,
who did grow up to be an artist

For Elizabeth —
This is a true story!
William Sleator
4·1·02

<<one

<<**At my funeral**, everybody said it was such a shame I had to die that way. Mrs. Hazelton, who ran over me, was too upset to come. Mom and Dad, who were subdued but not crying, told her husband that his wife wasn't to blame. What could she do, they said, when I ran out into the dark street without looking, right in front of her car?

I died instantly. All I was aware of was the shriek of the tires and the brief, heavy impact. Right away, I was floating upward, being pulled into the great white light.

And then the voice came, like a deep bell ringing inside my head. *Watch carefully, Peter*, said the voice. *There might be something important here for later.*

Suddenly I could see the church, the child's coffin, the religious service. It was sort of like watching it on TV, from above. But I was also right there in the middle of it, able to hear any conversation I wanted. Naturally I was most curious about Mom and Dad and Mr. Hazelton. "Peter always acted without thinking," Mom said after the funeral, sighing, her hand on her belly. She was expecting her first natural child.

Dad nodded. "It was his own fault."

It didn't surprise me to hear them say that. But it made me feel like crying, and I would have cried if I'd had eyes to cry with.

Then I was back inside the light. The voice came again. *Listen carefully, Peter. You are not permanently dead yet.*

"Huh? Then where am I?"

You have a chance to go back and fix things. You will remember everything that's going to happen. You can go back to any moment you choose before your death. If you are very careful and clever, you may be able to prevent your death. But you can't just not run out into the street. Once the critical moment is reached, you will be caught in it, as you were before. The changes you make have to prevent that. Do you understand?

"You mean . . . once I get upset and start to run, I'll *have* to run out into the street—even though I know the car will kill me?"

Correct. You have to fix things more deeply. Your emotions are as much a solid fact as the car being there. You have a period of up to twelve hours here before going back. Make good use of that time. When you are ready to go back, call for me. Your twelve-hour period is starting now.

"And that's it? This is the only chance I get?"

After you fail to fix your life, you will then be permanently dead like the others, with no hope.

"Are you saying that most people can't fix it so they stay alive? Does everybody get to do this?"

You now have eleven hours, fifty-nine minutes, and thirty seconds to plan your attempt. Call me when you are ready. You will then tell me to which moment you wish to be returned.

That was all it said. I thought for a while. It took me about ten minutes to decide what I could do to prevent my death. I didn't want to wait twelve hours. I wanted to go back right away and make it work this time. I missed being alive. I missed my projects.

I even missed my parents. A month and a half ago, they had told me I was adopted—and that Mom was going to have her own baby now. I was so stunned I didn't know what to think, except that it was all bad. My own parents hadn't wanted me, and now the ones I had always thought were my real parents weren't, and they were going to have their own child. Where did that put me? I was still trying to get used to it.

But that didn't mean I didn't want to go back. I missed everything. I even missed stupid ordinary things I'd never thought about, like the taste of toothpaste. I wanted my teeth back, I wanted my body back, I wanted my life back.

"I'm ready," I said.

There was a brief pause. Then the voice said, *So soon?*

"Yes. I know exactly what to do."

You are very sure?

"Yes! I thought about it a lot."

To which moment do you wish to be returned?

"Two A.M., the night before I died."

So be it. Your attempt now begins.

And then there I was, inside my body again, in bed in my room in the middle of the night. It felt wonderful.

But if I didn't act fast, I'd be dead again in less than twenty-four hours.

<<TWO

<<**TOMOFFOW, May 11**, was the surprise for my parents that I had worked on for so long. And right afterward, I had died.

It all started on the last day of March, when Mom came home with the news that she was going to have a baby. She and Dad hugged each other, and I was happy, too—until they both turned to me with the same funny expression.

"We have to tell you now, Peter," Mom said, her tone strangely hesitant. "We adopted you. We thought we couldn't have our own children, so God let us choose you."

It felt like a punch in the gut. They expected me to be excited about the new baby, but now all I could feel was how in one instant my whole life had been ripped out from under me. I knew they would love the baby more than me.

I mumbled something and ran up to my room, fighting tears. They would be disappointed in me, angry. But I couldn't help the way I felt.

Mom had always made wonderful cookies and cut my hair herself. Dad took me fishing and gave me baseball caps and let me help him rake the leaves.

But after Mom got pregnant, she would say, "Your neck is too skinny, and you're dark around the eyes like a raccoon."

And I wondered if Dad was joking when he said, "If you don't get better grades or learn how to hit a ball, we can always take you back to the orphanage."

I wanted them to love me, I wanted them to be proud of me, and sometimes they were. But after Mom found out she was going to have a baby, when I was eleven, I could never do anything right.

That was when I decided I had to prove to them that I was a really neat kid, after all.

I was terrible in math and lousy at sports. English I could deal with. My best subject was art. I could draw better than anybody in the class. I would look at something—a chair, a puppy, the view from the window at school—pick up a pencil and quickly make a drawing, and it would look like the real thing.

"Our new project is to make papier-mâché marionettes," Miss Lilly, the art teacher, had announced almost four weeks before my accident. Kurt Meyer, the big athlete at the next table, groaned. But I was excited. I made two puppets in the time it took everybody else to make one. And mine were more colorful and detailed and wildly grotesque—an alien and a scary clown. I even had time to paint a set.

My smart friend, Eloise, said, "Those puppets are amazing, Peter. I don't know how you do it."

Kurt Meyer's puppet was supposed to be a sitting cat, just three lumps stuck together, the least work he could do. He and his jock friends watched me working so hard and whispered and laughed. I did my best to ignore it, but it got to me.

I asked Mr. Martin, my shop teacher, if I could make a puppet stage, and he thought it was a great idea. There weren't a lot of extra materials, so it had to be simple. It was just an open rectangle of two-by-fours, with a Masonite floor and a Masonite backdrop the same size as the set. I made a curtain that I could open by hand and a scaffold above the front of the stage to hang a piece of cloth from, to hide the puppeteer. I didn't tell Mom and Dad about it. I wanted to surprise them and show them

I was clever and lovable, after all, even though I was adopted and they were going to have a new baby.

And now it was 2 A.M. the night before I was going to put on the puppet show for Mom and Dad. And I knew that after the show I would run out into the street, and Mrs. Hazelton would run over me, and I would die.

But now I could fix it so it wouldn't happen.

Unless it was all just a dream, and the accident and the white light and the voice had never happened. If that was the case, I could get in big trouble for what I was about to do.

Should I or shouldn't I? I tried not to groan.

But the "dream" had been more clear and vivid than any I'd ever had, especially the part about getting killed and the sensation of having no body. Impossible as it seemed, it *felt* so real. I was just making up excuses because I was scared about what I had to do now.

I sat up in bed, listening hard. I got up and slowly opened the door, then crept quietly across the small hallway in my pajamas, past the door of Mom and Dad's room. Dad always slept deeply after working all day in the printing factory—as much as he showered, he could never really get the smell of the ink off him. Now that Mom was pregnant, she slept soundly, too. Still, I went very slowly down the stairs, close to the wall so the boards wouldn't creak.

I didn't dare turn on the light in the dark kitchen.

I could hardly see and bumped the stool against the refrigerator. I froze, my heart pounding.

There was no sound from upstairs. I slowly maneuvered the stool under the cabinet and climbed up onto it. I managed to get an empty peanut-butter jar from the top shelf without dropping anything. Still on the stool, I unscrewed the sugar canister, poured sugar into the peanut-butter jar with the sugar dipper, and screwed the canister top back on. I got down and put the stool back and unlocked the back door. Outside, I pulled the door carefully shut and made sure not to let the screen door bang.

It was a cool spring night, but I was sweating in my pajamas. It wasn't going to be easy at the Hazeltons'.

They lived four houses away. I squeezed through the hedges that separated the backyards, not wanting to risk being seen on the sidewalk in front. Luckily they didn't have a garage, or else I wouldn't have been able to do what I was about to do. I pushed through the last hedge into their yard and then stopped, my hopes tumbling.

A downstairs light was on.

I didn't know what to do. Maybe they were all asleep and had just forgotten to turn the light off. But it was also possible that somebody was still awake downstairs and might notice what I was doing to their car. Did I dare to risk it anyway?

I had no choice. It would be terrible getting caught

vandalizing their car, but it would be worse being killed by it tomorrow.

If it hadn't all been a dream.

Stop thinking that! I silently ordered myself.

Crouching, so I'd be hidden behind the car, I moved across the wet grass. As I approached the car, I saw that the opening to the gas tank was not on this side. It had to be on the other side, the side facing the house, right next to the window with the light on.

I paused. What if I got caught?

But I had to do this. Still bent over, I hurried around to the other side of the car, just under the window. I didn't look behind me, I didn't look up at the window. I unscrewed the gas-tank cap and dumped in the sugar, then screwed the cap on again and scurried back around the car and out of the yard.

I had done it! And no one saw me. I was safe now, as long as I could get back inside the house and upstairs without waking Mom or Dad.

I had fixed it so I wouldn't die tomorrow. Sugar in the gas tank is lousy for the engine; the car can't be driven until it's repaired. Even if I got upset again and ran out into the street, the Hazeltons' car wouldn't—couldn't—be there to run over me. It hadn't been that difficult at all.

So why had the voice said that other people failed to fix their lives?

<<Three

<<Mom and Dad, I have something to show you," I said the next night after supper. "It's in the basement."

They looked up at me from the TV. "In the basement?" Dad said. He didn't sound excited; he sounded suspicious.

"Something I've been working on," I said, practically hopping with excitement. "Please? Hurry up!"

Mr. Martin had driven me home with the puppet stage that afternoon, while Dad was at the factory and Mom was grocery shopping. I had carefully set it all up, with the big blue cloth draped over the two-by-fours to hide me, a gooseneck lamp pointed down at the stage, and two chairs in front for the audience. I had done a great job with the puppets, the set, and the stage—Miss Lilly and Mr. Martin both said so, and so did Eloise, who never lied. Mom and Dad would have to be impressed with me.

What had happened last time was some kind of accident, a mistake. Maybe my acting hadn't been good enough or something. But now I had more practice. It would be better this time. I *knew* it.

Dad stood up and reluctantly turned off the TV. "I'm coming back up at eight to watch the game," he said.

It was twenty to eight. "That's enough time," I said. "Come on. Hurry! Please?"

They looked at each other in surprise when they saw the stage. "Where on earth did you get this?" Mom said.

"I built it all by myself," I said proudly. "It's my own design."

They looked at each other again, and Dad lifted his eyebrows. They *would* be impressed this time, I was sure.

"Sit down. Take your seats and watch the show," I said. "Come on. What are you waiting for?"

They sat down, looking uncomfortable. But once they saw how great the puppets were, and the set, they would have to enjoy it this time, they couldn't help it.

I stepped behind the stage, hidden by the cloth. I turned on the stage light. I held the controls of the clown puppet in my right hand, and with my left I pulled open the curtain, saying "Ta-da!"

The clown was beautiful—and frightening. His hair was a metal pot scrubber. He had a big blue nose, triangular yellow eyes, and curving red lips. His costume was baggy, red-and-white-striped, and his gigantic shoes flapped when he walked. The set was the inside of a circus arena, the people's heads and eyes roughly drawn, but giving the effect of a huge audience.

The clown waved and said, "Hello, folks!" and then tripped and fell over his own feet, which was supposed to be funny, but nobody laughed. I was nervous, so my hands were sweaty and shaking. The clown trembled as he got up.

I picked up the alien puppet control with my left hand, and the alien puppet slithered onto the stage. It was like an octopus with a bird's head. The tentacles were cheap rubber snakes. The body glittered with scales made out of green sequins. The big bird's beak bulged with wicked, sharp teeth.

"What's that thing?" cried the clown. "It's not part of the show! Help! But the audience is just laughing!"

"I'm from the planet Ja-Ja-Bee," the alien croaked, "and I'm hungry, and I'm going to eat this whole audience, starting with you. And no one will stop me because they'll think it's all an act!" The alien lunged at the clown—and as he lunged, two of his strings got tangled, making him harder to manipulate. This hadn't happened the first time.

I was scared now, but I still remembered what the clown had to say. "You can't do that!" the clown squealed and started to run. Then he stopped. "But I can't just run away! I have to save the audience!" he bravely announced. And he turned to face the alien.

The fight between the clown and the alien was the hardest part. And now the alien was tangled, and I was more nervous than before because last time I hadn't known I might be going to die in the next ten minutes. My hands were shaking. I remembered the feeling of the car hitting me. The alien reached out for the clown—and I dropped the alien onto the stage, controls and all.

All I could do was reach down and pull it back up again, blushing. I continued the fight, feeling my heart thudding. I had to use one of my left-hand fingers, holding the alien control, to move the clown's leg string, which was very tricky. The clown kicked out with his foot at the alien's beak—at least I did that part right.

"Argh!" the alien screamed. "The smell of that foot! It's too disgusting! I can't stand it!" And the alien died, collapsing in a heap. I draped his controls awkwardly over the back of the stage—hoping they wouldn't fall down again—so I could work the clown with two hands.

The clown faced the audience, lifting both his arms, and he shrugged sadly. "I just saved the world—and nobody will ever know it because they think it was only an act." He wiped a tear away. I pulled the curtain closed.

There was no sound from the audience. I felt terrible about what had happened—last time I hadn't dropped a puppet. I made myself step around to the front of the stage, feeling sheepish, not proud at all. But I still couldn't keep from saying, "Well? What did you think?"

Mom looked at Dad. He was glowering, his arms folded. "How much time you spend doing this kind of stuff? Messing with sequins and sewing little costumes?" he asked me.

My stomach went cold. It was happening the way it had before. The only change was that it was worse now, because I had dropped a puppet. "Couldn't you see what I did?" I asked him. "The stage construction? The way the puppet controls work? You didn't even notice how—"

"Waste of time," Mom said, picking up Dad's attitude.

Dad sighed deeply. "Why can't you be like other boys?" he said, angry and disappointed in me. "Why aren't you out there playing baseball and football instead of messing around with *dolls*?"

"You couldn't see they're not dolls? They're marionettes, like alive!"

He ignored me. "And you can't even work them without dropping them," he said with contempt.

They weren't impressed this time either. It was worse than before. They were acting just like the popular kids at school, like Kurt Meyer, who made fun of me for liking art and not sports. I felt like there was nowhere in the world where I could be safe, where I could be who I really am. And what would it be like when the baby came? The coldness in my stomach was suddenly hot, a burning pain that had to be released. "I'm sorry I'm me! I can't help being me!" I shouted. I turned and pounded up the stairs.

It was just like the voice had said. Once you reached a certain point, you couldn't change things—it was programmed to go this way. Here I was, miserable and humiliated and hurting worse than if Dad had hit me, running outside without thinking.

But at least this time Mrs. Hazelton wouldn't be driving her car right past our house the moment I ran into the street.

She wasn't. The taxi that had been behind Mrs. Hazelton was going faster now. It hit me harder than she had.

I died for the second time.

<<FOUR

<<**YOUR ELEVEN-HOUR**-*and-forty-seven-minute period is starting now, Peter,* the voice said. *Call me when you are ready to go back again. I suggest you use all the time available to make your plan.*

I didn't have a body, but I was still reeling from the shock of being run over a second time. "I have another chance?" I gasped. "Do I have more chances after that?"

There was no answer. The voice was gone.

I had used thirteen minutes of the twelve hours last time, which left me eleven hours and forty-seven minutes.

So now what was I going to do? I had gotten rid of Mrs. Hazelton's car, but a taxi had taken its place, and I had no idea how to get rid of the taxi. It seemed hopeless.

The voice had said something before about how I had to fix things more deeply—that my emotions were as much a solid fact as the car being there. So, if I couldn't make sure no car would come along, what could I do to make sure my emotions wouldn't force me to run into the street? I had been through it twice now; it was obviously programmed to happen after Mom and Dad saw the puppet show.

But I couldn't just control my emotions by willpower. I had spent so much time and worked so hard, and I believed the stage and the sets and the puppets really were wonderful. And then Mom tells me I'm wasting my time, and Dad accuses me of playing with dolls. How could I *not* be upset?

If Mom and Dad had never seen the puppet show, then I wouldn't have gotten upset, and I would never have run out into the street.

Now I was thinking even harder. What if I did something really radical, like go way, way back and not make the puppets at all? Then none of this would ever happen.

But that idea really bothered me. I had gotten so much pleasure from creating it all; it had come so naturally to me. And Eloise and Miss Lilly and Mr. Martin all thought the puppets, the stage, and the set were beautiful.

I pushed that thought aside. Doing the puppet show for Mom and Dad had resulted directly in my death. It had happened two times now and seemed to be unavoidable. I had loved making the puppets, but if I wanted to live, I had to give them up.

Maybe I could do something different to impress Mom and Dad, something I was sure they would like.

Like what? Do better in math? Make my neck thicker and the skin around my eyes lighter? Play baseball after school instead of drawing and making puppets? I shuddered. Then I remembered the feeling of being hit by the car and shuddered even more.

Was it possible there was something they would like that I wouldn't hate?

I began putting together a plan. I thought a lot more slowly and carefully than I had the last time—this might be my last chance, and that was really scary. Still, I didn't take the whole eleven hours and forty-seven minutes. I called the voice before it told me my time was up.

Are you sure you are ready? the voice asked me.

"Yes, I'm sure. I planned a lot more carefully this time. Dates and everything."

You understand, this time you may be dead forever.

"I know that! I'm ready. I want to go back."

To which moment do you wish to be returned?

"Almost four weeks before I died. Monday, April 16, at seven A.M., the day we began making the puppets."

So be it. Your second attempt now begins.

And there I was, lying in bed on Monday morning, back inside my body again.

<<five

"<<peter! Time to get up!" Mom called.

Mom served us breakfast. She did all the work but hardly ate anything. She often felt sick in the mornings now, because of being pregnant. Dad fussed over her. She had to be very careful.

I didn't want anything to go wrong either. Actually I was looking forward to having a little sister or brother. I even felt I could love it. But I also knew they would love the baby more than me, because it was really their own. I still felt a pang every time I thought about being adopted. It would have been different if I'd known all along, instead of having it dropped on me when Mom got pregnant. But I was afraid to talk about my real feelings with Mom and Dad.

"Our new project is to make papier-mâché mario-nettes," Miss Lilly said in art class that day. Kurt Meyer, at the table next to me, groaned.

I groaned, too. He looked over at me, surprised.

Miss Lilly did, too. "Did you say something, Peter?" she asked, not smiling.

I could feel my pulse picking up. From this moment on, my life would veer off in a different direction. It was scary, but also exciting.

"Well, er . . . if somebody really didn't want to make puppets, could he do something else? Please?"

I noticed Kurt Meyer nodding in agreement.

"But puppets are the kind of thing I thought you es-pecially would enjoy, Peter," Miss Lilly said.

She was right; I hated not making my puppets. But this was my plan for staying alive. I had thought care-fully and knew what to say next. "I'm more interested in drawing," I said. "I could draw a cartoon. You know, in a flip book, where each page has a picture a tiny bit differ-ent from the last one. When you flip through it, it looks like it's moving." Then I added, "I could draw a man hit-ting a home run." Dad might like the flip book if it was about baseball.

"That might be kind of cool," Kurt Meyer whispered.

"This really isn't like you, Peter," Miss Lilly said. "You're more imaginative than—"

"A phone call for Miss Lilly," said a voice through the loudspeaker.

"Be right there. Behave yourselves, class."

This announcement hadn't happened the last time. Were other things already starting to change because I had changed my own life? Or was that crazy?

As soon as Miss Lilly was out of the room, Kurt Meyer was over at my table. Ordinarily he would never have stooped to talk to me, because I was such a nothing. "Hey, Pete," he said. "Maybe I could help you make that flip book. I mean, you don't know how to play baseball. I could be, like, your technical advisor or something."

I didn't like Kurt Meyer. He had tried to get me to work with him when we did our last project, making picture storybooks, four weeks earlier. I had said Miss Lilly wouldn't like it, and he called me a teacher's pet. Mom and Dad had barely even looked at the book I made. They were more interested in the big fire at Robinson's Department Store that had happened the day I brought the book home.

"I have to do good in art," Kurt Meyer was saying now. "I have to do better in all my classes, or they'll kick me off the teams. So I need a good recommendation from Lilly, that I *applied* myself. If I worked with you, and the project came out good, that could help me a lot."

Maybe I should work with Meyer this time. Okay, so I didn't like him. But he was exactly the kind of guy Dad wanted me to be. If I could get to be friends with him, that might impress Dad. "I'll think about it."

"Think fast, Pete," he said roughly. "What are you going to lose? Just ask her as soon as she comes back. She'll buy it if it comes from you, but not from me. Anyway, you really do need my help with the baseball."

Why not? If Meyer owed me a favor, maybe he would help me with Dad. "Okay, enough already, I'll *do* it!"

"Now, where were we?" Miss Lilly said when she came back. "Oh, yes, Peter and his baseball flip book."

"Please, Miss Lilly, I need somebody to work with me," I said quickly. "So I can get the moves right. Somebody who knows about baseball, like Kurt."

Kurt Meyer's hand shot up. "I'll do it," he said. "That could be my project, too, instead of a puppet."

Miss Lilly frowned. "Just a minute, Kurt," she said. She turned back to me and sighed. "This isn't like you, Peter," she said again. "But if that's what you really want to do, okay. And if he needs you to help him, Kurt, you may. Baseball *is* your field of expertise, after all."

"Why are you making a baseball flip book instead of a puppet?" Eloise asked me after school.

"I . . . I don't feel like making a puppet," I said lamely.

"But you'd make such a beautiful puppet! You're a genius at exactly that kind of stuff. And you're working with that horrible Kurt Meyer!" She sighed, puzzled. "Is there something you're not telling me?"

I hadn't told her that I was adopted and that Mom was pregnant, or about how much I needed to impress Mom and Dad. And I hadn't told her about dying and getting two other chances.

Eloise was smart, and she was my best friend. If there was anybody I could talk to about this whole frightening situation, it would be her. And I needed advice—I had botched my chances the last two times.

But for some reason I couldn't tell her. Maybe I was afraid she'd think I was crazy. "I have to get home early," I said, and hurried away.

<<six

<<**what are you** so down-in-the-mouth about, Pete?" Dad asked me at breakfast the next day.

"I'm not down-in-the-mouth," I said. "I'm working on a project with Kurt Meyer, the best athlete in the class."

Dad raised his eyebrows as though he didn't believe me. "You're friends with somebody like that?"

In art class I drew one boring picture after another, each one hardly different from the last. And Kurt Meyer corrected me, over and over and over again.

I looked at the other kids and sighed. I thought about the alien and the clown puppets, and how much better they had been than the crude ones the other kids were making. It was like a physical pain, not to be building those puppets. I even dreamed about them.

I felt so unhappy, I began to wonder about this plan. Maybe I would live this time. But what kind of life was this, when I knew exactly what I was aching to do, and I couldn't do it?

But it was too late to turn back now. I had already changed everything.

And then it got worse.

The Monday of the second week, Meyer was nastier than usual. "You're drawing it wrong on purpose," he accused me.

"Look, I'm trying," I said. "What's the matter with you today, anyway?"

"My little brother fell off a swing yesterday and broke his shoulder, and my parents say I was pushing too hard. They're grounding me for a month."

I didn't feel sorry for him; I was glad he was in trouble, but I said, "Oh, that's too bad."

"Can it," he said. "You'll never know how to draw a batter until you know how to hit a ball. Tomorrow you start playing in the baseball game we have after school. I need that recommendation from Lilly."

"What are you sulking about now, Pete?" Dad asked me the next morning. "You worried about something these days?"

He was pretending to care, but I knew it really made him angry when I didn't act cheerful about everything. "I'm fine, I'm fine, okay?" I said. "Meyer asked me to play baseball after school. I guess I'll be playing with them every day now. Doesn't that make you happy?"

"It doesn't seem to make you happy." He frowned at me. "I wonder how long it'll last."

It was like he was saying it wouldn't last. "You'll see, I'll be there every day," I insisted.

"Uh-huh," he said, and turned to Mom. "You feeling okay, Gert?" he asked her.

She put down the cereal she was serving. "I need to go to the bathroom again," she said, looking pale.

"I'll help you," Dad said, getting up quickly.

I finished breakfast alone and got ready for school. Mom and Dad never understood me. And I was dreading the baseball game that afternoon. As usual, I was too preoccupied to think about clearing the table.

I struck out every time I was at bat. They told me to keep my eye on the ball, but the one time I did connect, it was a foul. When the other team was up, Meyer put me way, way out in right field, where balls were hardly ever hit. I stood there in the warm spring sunshine, praying no balls would come near me. And then a ball came directly at me, and I flubbed the catch and had to run after the ball. But I didn't throw it hard or fast enough. The batter got a home run because of me.

"I'll do better tomorrow, I know I will," I said to Meyer. "And maybe I'll draw better because of this."

"I hope you do," he said, disgusted with me. He walked off with his dumb jock friends.

"I played baseball this afternoon with the guys," I told Dad at supper.

"How did it go? Did you score?" he asked me.

I was sure he was being sarcastic. "No, I didn't *score*," I said, sighing. "But I'm getting better. They told me I was. I'm going to play every day."

"Fine," Dad said, turning away as though he didn't care. Would anything I did ever impress him?

He was in a bad mood because he had just paid a lot of money to get the car fixed—he had forgotten to change the oil. That had happened in my original life, too.

In art class the next day, Meyer made me draw the batter over and over again. I hadn't expected a jock to be such a perfectionist about art. "It's because *you* can't do it yourself. Watch the other guys this afternoon, and then *draw* it," he said. "Understand?"

That afternoon I concentrated hard on watching the guys at bat. And when I was up at bat, I hit the ball, and it wasn't a foul. But it was a pop fly, and somebody caught it before I got close to first base. Still, I had done a little better. Meyer didn't say anything to me afterward.

But in school the next day, he said, "Maybe we can keep a couple of these drawings now." That's when I realized that he was the boss of this project. I was doing all the work, but he was the one in control.

And Dad could tell from my manner and expression that I wasn't doing well at baseball. He could see that I was unhappy. And he didn't like it. "I don't know what you're so down-in-the-mouth about, Pete," he said. "We give you a good home, and your mother always makes good food for you, and we don't make you sell papers for your spending money or ask you to help around the house. So don't sulk so much. Things won't be so easy for you after the new baby comes."

I was trying to be the kind of person Dad wanted, and it wasn't working. It was worse than before. Maybe I could never be that imaginary person he was always telling me I should be.

On the Friday that the art project was over, and the other kids had finished their puppets, Miss Lilly examined the flip book. "Well, it does look very accurate. Did Kurt really help? You couldn't have done it without him?"

I nodded automatically. "Yes, he helped me a lot."

"Okay, Kurt, I'll give you that recommendation."

As soon as we left, I said, "I helped you out. Maybe you could come over tonight when I show this to my parents? Please? It would make a big difference."

"I'm grounded because of my brother, remember?" he said. "And, uh, I guess you don't need to come to practice anymore." He sounded a little sheepish when he said it, but I knew he couldn't really feel bad about dropping me.

I didn't know what I was going to tell Dad about being kicked out of baseball practice. But at least I had the flip book now, and it wasn't bad, if you cared about baseball. Maybe Mom and Dad would like it.

Eloise didn't, when I showed it to her after school. "Is that all?" she said, shaking her head. "You could have made a really beautiful puppet."

I hated hearing that. "But I worked so hard on this!" I protested. "I put up with Meyer. You just don't understand this because you can't draw at all."

"Just because you're *sometimes* a great artist doesn't mean you *always* have to be a temperamental baby!" she said, and stalked off.

"So how was baseball?" Dad asked me after supper.

"I don't feel like talking about it," I said.

He sighed. "Sulking again. They dropped you, right?"

"It wasn't like that. Look at this. I made it."

I got out the flip book and showed it to him. "What is this? I don't get it," he said. "Do you know what this is, Gert?" he asked Mom.

She shook her head, barely looking up from her knitting, not interested in what I had made.

"Watch," I said. I tried to remind myself that the animation was smooth and gave an almost lifelike impression of a man hitting a ball.

I held the book up so Dad could see and flipped through it. The pitcher threw the ball; it whizzed through the air fast; the batter swung and connected, turning his upper body. He flung the bat behind him and took off. The pictures followed the ball as it flew out of the stadium.

Dad stared at it, surprised. "Hey, let me do that," he said. He flipped through it himself.

"Look at this, Gert," he said, and did it for Mom.

I held my breath. Was he going to be impressed? Maybe even proud of me? Was it possible that all these weeks of doing the same boring drawings over and over again, suffering humiliation on the baseball field, and being bossed around by Kurt Meyer, were going to pay off?

Mom looked away from her knitting long enough to watch the flip book. But she didn't say anything.

She had grown up on a farm and cared only about practical things.

"Can't you see it's a cartoon?" I explained, trying to be patient. Didn't they understand *anything*? "It's entertainment. It's a drawing that looks like it's alive. I did it myself. It's not easy to make that effect."

Dad flipped through it another time. Then he casually dropped it onto the coffee table. "It's something, I guess," he said. "But it sure isn't entertainment. Same thing over and over again. If you were on a team, and we could watch you play, now that would be entertainment."

My heart sank. But, in a way, he and Eloise were right. The flip book was a paltry thing compared to the puppets. I wished now more than ever that I had made them.

Dad turned toward the TV, then looked quickly back at me. "And you can stop sulking," he said.

"But I thought . . . maybe you'd like it."

"How long did it take you to make that thing that it takes one second to look at?" he asked me. "Don't tell me. I know. Weeks and weeks." He sighed and shook his head. "And all that time you could have been out there really playing the game, instead of making that thing."

"But I *was* playing baseball. Every afternoon. I—"

"Bragging again. They kicked you off, didn't they?

You can't lie to me. And wipe that expression off your face." He shook his finger at me. "I'm tired of your moping and bragging and wasting your time on useless, peculiar things, instead of doing something real. You better shape up before the new baby comes. And you better be nice to him, too."

That was too much. I already loved the new baby, and it wasn't even born yet. And he was accusing me of being mean to it and telling me I was no good because I made a cartoon, by hand, that really moved—and wasn't good at baseball. "I love the new baby! How can you say I don't?" I said, almost crying. "I'm sorry I like to draw instead of playing sports! I'm not doing it on purpose." I was shouting now. "I'm sorry I'm me! I can't help being me!" I turned and ran out of the house.

I hadn't escaped this time either. Here I was, miserable and humiliated and running. And I couldn't stop.

But this time was a little different. I'd made a bigger change in my life, and I'd also been through this moment two times before. This time I was thinking. I hadn't done anything to stop Mrs. Hazelton's car, and anyway the taxi was right behind it. And somehow I was able to turn and stay on the sidewalk. Mrs. Hazelton's car went past, and then the taxi.

Was it possible I *wasn't* going to die?

It wasn't. Headlights blinded me as an old pickup veered up onto the sidewalk.

But in the last instant before the impact, I was thinking: Maybe it'll be okay. Maybe I have a lot more chances after this one.

I died for the third time.

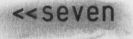

<<seven

<<**your final five**-*hour-and-two-minute period is starting now, Peter,* the voice said. *I strongly urge you to use all that time.*

"Final? You mean I don't get any more chances after this one? This is *it*? And I only have *five hours*?"

I suggest you plan very, very carefully.

I sensed the voice was leaving. "Wait!" I said desperately. "If this is my last chance, then you have to answer some questions. Please? Why is this happening to me? Does it happen to everybody? And who are you, anyway?"

I cannot answer those questions. It is better for you not to know the answers. I can only tell you that this is your last chance.

I was panicking. The first time I had gotten the car out of the way, but a taxi had taken its place. The second time I had tried to change *myself* instead of the accident. It hadn't worked. I had tried to be good at baseball, I had tried to be the kind of son Mom and Dad would be proud of, and I found out that I couldn't be that person. What else could I do? It was hopeless.

But I couldn't just give up. My last life had been almost too miserable to bear. But I still had another chance to make a good life. I had to give it one last try.

And I had to do something else: make the puppet show. I knew now that it wasn't fair to me *not* to do it. The puppets were a part of me that had to be expressed. I refused to give in, to waste my life on a mechanical flip book or on the baseball field. Painting and sculpting and making shows were my favorite things in the world. If I couldn't do them, I wouldn't really be me, really alive.

I kept frantically looking for my watch, and then seeing nothing because I had no body here. Five hours wasn't much time. How fast was it going? My mind was a confused mess. The more desperate I felt, the less logically I could think.

Where was the answer? I thought about Mom and Dad, what they liked, what they didn't like. What they didn't like was easy, especially what they didn't like about me. What they liked was a lot harder. And I knew now that I couldn't just try to *be* what they thought they wanted me to be—it wouldn't work, and I couldn't do it anyway.

But Mom was right about how I acted without thinking, rushed into things. Maybe they were right about some other things, too. Maybe Dad *wasn't* just being nasty when he laid into me about my moods and my behavior around the house.

Was it possible I was on to something?

And Meyer. Was he really so bad, after all? He had been a perfectionist about the flip book. It meant a lot of work for me, but it had impressed me, too. I hadn't expected him to care so much about an art project.

So if he wasn't all that bad, could it be something *I* was doing that made him and some of the other guys laugh at me? And that made Dad so hostile to me?

Eloise said that being a great artist didn't mean you had to be a temperamental baby. Was I a temperamental baby?

If I'd had a heart, it would have been pounding now, I was so excited. How could I use these new thoughts to change things so that people—especially Mom and Dad—would appreciate me for who I really was?

That was what it all boiled down to: I had to make Mom and Dad want me—even though I was adopted and now they were going to have their own child. And I had to do it before the baby came; after that, it would be too late. I was going to have to be more clever than I had ever been in my eleven years.

I thought, I planned, I concentrated, aware every second of the clock ticking away. Maybe my new ideas wouldn't work. But they were different from anything I had thought of the last two times.

Your time is up now, Peter, the voice said. *To which moment do you wish to be returned?*

I wasn't ready. I didn't even know how far back to go. "I need another hour!" I begged, more panicked now.

To which moment do you wish to be returned?

I didn't know. I should have made up my mind about this crucial point first. Now I had to make a snap decision. Should I go back to the day we started making the puppets? Was four weeks enough time for what I had to do?

Your time is up, Peter. If you don't tell me now, I will return you to the same moment as last time.

But why *not* go back farther, just to be sure I'd have enough time? "No, don't!" I shouted. "Send me back to four wecks *before* the last time, almost eight weeks ago."

So be it. Your final attempt now begins.

And there I was, lying in bed, inside my body again. It always felt good to have my body back. But this time it didn't feel as good as it had before.

Because this time I knew it was my last chance.

<<eight

<<It was darker outside than the last two times, and the room was colder. I had gone back into winter.

I looked at the calendar. It was my habit to cross off the days, and today was Monday, March 19. Almost eight weeks from now—on Friday, May 11—I would die, unless I could make some very deep changes in my life.

"Peter! Time to get up!" Mom called.

I got out of bed, shivering in my pajamas. The bathroom would be freezing, but I couldn't dawdle. We all had to share it, and Mom might be sick. . . .

And then it hit me. She didn't know she was pregnant. She hadn't found out until the last day of March. I remembered the date precisely; it was such an important occasion—that was the day they told me I was adopted.

I knew Mom was going to have a baby, and she didn't.

When I was planning my strategy, I hadn't thought about how I would know what was going to happen in the future, things Mom and Dad couldn't possibly know. Not just about the new baby, but about other things, too. How could I use that?

I dressed quickly; my mind whirled with possibilities.

Mom was about to climb up on a kitchen stool. "Hold on, Mom. Let me help you with that," I said. She paused, and so I quickly got up onto the stool. "What do you want?"

"That jar over there on the right."

I got it down and handed it to her. "Uh, thanks, Peter," she said, puzzled.

"What was that all about?" Dad said.

"Oh, I just think Mom should be taking good care of herself these days," I said. And I was thinking that in twelve days they would find out she was pregnant. "Sit down, Mom," I said. "Take it easy. I can serve myself."

I usually never helped around the house at all. "What kind of an act is this?" Dad said.

"It's not an act," I said, spooning oatmeal into my

bowl from the pot on the stove. "I'm just trying to pamper Mom a little, for a change."

I dug in. The sudden change back to cold weather had given me more of an appetite than usual. Plus I wanted to try for more than one bowl this morning, since they thought I was too skinny. I ate a bowl and a half. They both noticed, especially because I got up to serve it myself—usually Mom asked me if I wanted more, and I said I didn't.

It was cold on the walk to school, the trees were bare, and snow was melting on the lawns and in the gutters.

I was almost quivering with tension. I couldn't stop thinking about how this was my last chance, and every action would lead either to my staying alive or dying. I felt jumpy and irritable.

"Our next four-week project will be to make picture books," Miss Lilly said in art class. "Each student will write a story and illustrate it."

Kurt Meyer groaned—he always groaned when she announced our next project.

When we did this project before, I made a book about a haunted house. Mom and Dad had barely glanced at it; they were more interested in the news about the big fire at Robinson's Department Store the day I brought the book home. Eloise and Miss Lilly had loved the drawings, at least.

I decided to do something different this time, to start the changes going four weeks earlier. And because the changes were starting earlier, they might end up being bigger. I wanted them to be bigger. I *needed* them to be bigger. The last three times had all ended up going wrong, especially the one just before this one.

Maybe I could use what I had learned about baseball then but do something more magical than a flip book that was just a copy of real life.

"Hey, pal, maybe we can work on our book together," Kurt Meyer said, just like he had said the first time Miss Lilly had announced the picture-book project. He knew I was the best artist in the class and that I could do most of the work and he would have to do hardly anything. I knew this now because of working on the flip book with him.

When he had asked me this the last time, I had meekly said Miss Lilly wouldn't like it, and he had made a face and said, "Teacher's pet! I'll find somebody else."

This time things were different. "No, thanks, Meyer," I said, tense and irritable and remembering how bossy he had been—and forgetting I had decided he might be an okay guy, after all. "Find somebody else to do all the work."

His mouth dropped open. Nobody talked to big, popular, star athlete Kurt Meyer like that! Especially not a nobody like me, who was good only at art. "Just wait'll gym class, jerk," he threatened me.

Gym would be torture. But at least he wasn't laughing at me or ridiculing me or ordering me around, like before.

And I knew something Meyer didn't know; I knew who was going to win the big basketball game against our arch rivals. I usually didn't pay attention to school sports, but this one I knew because it was the last and most important game of the season, and I remembered how happy I was when our class team—Meyer was the captain—lost.

For the rest of art class, I plotted out a baseball story for my book. The ideas came so fast that I almost finished the first draft before the period ended.

We played volleyball in gym. I got picked last, as always. I was on Meyer's team. He did everything to keep the ball away from me and to bump into me as roughly as possible. When the ball did fall into my hands, I flubbed it, and we lost the point and the game.

But this was only gym class. It wasn't as important as the final basketball game against Hanley on Wednesday.

"You flubbed that ball on purpose, you dumb jerk," Meyer said to me on the way out of the locker room.

"It's only gym class," I said, shrugging. "Too bad

you're going to lose the big basketball game with Hanley on Wednesday, twenty-five to two."

"Huh?" he said, stopping, surprised.

"And you won't even be the one to score," I added.

"What's gotten into you today, guts-for-brains?" he said, starting toward me. "You have a death wish?"

I scurried away from him in the crowded hallway.

I walked home with Eloise. She wasn't mad at me, because our fight about the nonexistent flip book hadn't happened yet—and now it never would.

Eloise was pretty in an odd way, with very pale red hair, and she was a better student than I was. She loved art, too, but she just couldn't draw. She thought I was kind of a genius at it, which is why we became friends.

"I never heard you talk to Kurt like you did today," she said. "Weren't you afraid he'd get you?"

"He did. He pushed me in gym." I smiled. "And then I told him his team is going to lose the game with Hanley on Wednesday, twenty-five to two."

"Why did you say something like that?" Eloise asked me. "You'll just look like a jerk when it doesn't happen."

"It's going to happen," I said, feeling my confidence soar. It was great being able to predict the future.

She pushed back her hair and peered at me. "What are you talking about?" she said.

"If I tried to explain, you wouldn't believe me," I said. "Just wait and see."

Eloise was looking at me strangely now. "You're different today," she said, as though different wasn't good.

Suddenly I didn't feel so confident. Maybe it hadn't been such a great idea to predict the future like this.

<<Nine

<<The morning after the game, I was so nervous I couldn't stay in bed. I had the oatmeal ready and the bread toasting by the time Mom and Dad came down. Mom smiled at me more warmly than I could ever remember. And now Dad didn't make any cracks about this being an act. "You sure are energetic these days," he said pleasantly, unfolding the paper.

Meyer was waiting for me in front of the school. He stood there staring hard at me as I approached. Was he going to hit me? I wanted to turn around and go home, but I couldn't. He didn't say anything until I got very close.

"How did you know that?" he said very softly.

My mouth was dry. "What . . . what happened?" I said.

"We lost twenty-five to two. I didn't score." I had never heard him sound like this before. He was trying to be calm, trying to hide his feelings, but it was clear that he was very upset. Was he scared? Scared of me? "How did you know?" he said again.

I remembered what Mom had said at my funeral about how I always acted without thinking. Doing the opposite—thinking before acting—was one of the ways I had decided to try to change, to fix my life this time. But I had forgotten that when I blurted out the future to Meyer. If I'd thought more, I would have realized that Meyer would want to know *how* I knew about the game. What could I tell him? Already I had gotten myself into a worse mess than last time.

Meyer was several inches taller than me and a lot stronger. He put his big hand on the back of my neck and gave it a painful squeeze. "Tell me, if you know what's good for you," he said, still speaking in that strange soft voice. It didn't seem to mean he was scared.

Kids walking past glanced at us and then looked the other way. Nobody wanted to interfere with Meyer.

"It just . . . it just came out of my mouth," I said. "When you told me I faked that flub in gym, I didn't think, I just opened my mouth, and it came out about the game."

"You expect me to believe that?" he said, still squeezing. "You expect me to believe you don't have some kind of method? You knew it in advance. That means you must know other things in advance, too. Things that could be real useful to me. Like what's going to be on the English quiz tomorrow."

English was his worst subject. Everybody knew he was in danger of flunking. If he didn't pass this test, he'd be kicked off the teams.

I squirmed away from his hand. "I won't talk unless you let go of me," I said.

He dropped his hand. "Talk."

"It's not like you think," I said, trying to sound confident and not scared. "It never happened to me before. Like I said, the words just came—"

The first bell rang. He lifted his hand abruptly, threateningly. "If it never happened before, then why did you sound so sure of yourself? You said it like you knew it was true. That means you have a way of knowing what's going to happen. I want to know what's going to be on the English quiz tomorrow. Meet me here after school and tell me. If you don't, you'll be in big trouble." He stared hard at me, not blinking. "Understand?"

<<TEN

<<**εloise was the** only person I could turn to for help. But how could she help me if I didn't tell her the truth? About everything.

She was in my homeroom. When they gave the results of the game during morning announcements, she turned and looked at me, raising her eyebrows. Now maybe she wouldn't think I was nuts when I explained.

We could talk during lunch. She smiled when we sat down. "Okay, how did you know about the game?"

"It's a long story." I started by telling her about being adopted, and Mom having her first natural child.

"Adopted? And they didn't tell you until your mother got pregnant?" Eloise said, looking concerned. "How did you feel?"

"Well, yeah, it was real hard," I admitted. "I'm still getting used to it. I wish I'd known all along. But . . . I'm happy about the baby," I said. "Even though I'm sure they'll love it more than me. I'm just afraid that after the baby comes, there's no hope they'll ever appreciate me for who I am and for what I'm good at."

"That *might* not be true . . ." she said. But she was just being kind. She knew about my problem with Mom and Dad.

"Well, anyway, it makes it even more important for them to understand me as soon as possible," I said. I started telling her about our next art project, puppets.

"Wait a minute," she said. "How do you know what—"

"Just listen." I told her everything—about Dad ridiculing me about the puppet show, about running out and getting hit by the car, about the light and the voice, and how I'd flubbed my first two chances and only had this one left.

"I don't know what to say," she said, shaking her head, looking a little dazed. "It's kind of too much."

"How else could I know about the game? How else could I know what's going to be on the English quiz tomorrow?"

"The English quiz? What about the English quiz?"

I sighed. "I made a big mistake telling Meyer about the game. Now he thinks I know everything that's going to happen. If he doesn't pass the English test, he'll be kicked off the teams. So he wants to know what's going to be on the English quiz, and if I don't tell him he's going to punch me around."

"*Do* you know?"

"Uh-huh. We have to write about—"

She lifted her hand to shush me. "I don't want to know. I just wanted to know if you knew." That was Eloise—she didn't want to know the test question in advance because it wouldn't be fair. Not that it would make any difference to her; she'd know the answer no matter what.

"Yeah, well, I do happen to remember it, because I was so relieved I knew the answer," I said. "But what do I tell Meyer? If I tell him the truth about the test, he'll never leave me alone again. He'll want to know the answers to everything, including a lot of stuff I really *don't* remember. But if I tell him the wrong answer, he'll think I lied to him, and he'll get kicked off the teams—and go on punishing me for a long, long time."

The good thing about Eloise was that she didn't waffle or say things like it was my own problem and she couldn't tell me what to do—like my parents would have done, and most other people, too. Eloise gave practical, specific solutions. "You can't tell him what's really going to be on the test," she said. "Then he'll make you his slave. You'll have to tell him something wrong, or nothing at all, and take the punishment until he stops."

I groaned.

"Sorry," she said. She thought for a moment. "You know, it might be a good idea to tell him what you just told me—about dying and coming back and all that."

"Tell *Meyer*?"

"Maybe he'll believe you, and then he'll understand why you knew about the game but don't know other things. But he probably won't believe you. He'll think you're crazy and keep away from you. And that's what you want."

"But I hate telling Meyer something so personal."

She shrugged. "You asked me. I think that's the best way to get rid of him. And be as realistic as possible about the details. That way there's a chance he might actually believe it. Maybe. Realistic details are what make people believe things they find hard to believe. And try to be calm and confident when you talk to him."

All day I worried about meeting Meyer after school. I had always avoided physical fights. How much was it going to hurt? And how much would Dad ridicule me if I came home with a black eye or missing teeth?

Meyer was waiting for me out in back. "Well, what's going to be on the quiz?" he said.

I said firmly, "I don't know."

He grabbed the front of my jacket. "So how did you know about the game?"

"Because I remember some things and not other things," I said, trying to keep my voice from shaking. "And I *don't* remember what was on the English test."

He frowned and pushed me roughly away. "What do you mean, remember? We're talking about the future."

So I told him about the puppet show and dying and the voice. Right away he was shaking his head in angry disbelief. "You expect me to believe that crud?" he said. He grabbed my jacket again. "What's on the English test?"

"I don't remember! Wait a minute! You're in my last life, too," I said, desperately trying to think of something to say that would appease him. Eloise had told me to be as realistic as possible. "Don't you want to know what happened then—and what's *not* going to happen now?"

"Huh?" He seemed confused, but curious.

I told him about my first try, how I had disabled Mrs. Hazelton's car, but a taxi had hit me instead. He dropped his hand from my jacket, listening. I told him about my second try, not making the puppets and making a baseball flip book with him instead. I told him how accurate he had been, making me draw it so many times—it was boring but it still kind of impressed me. I emphasized how much I missed making the puppets, how good they had been. "And then I showed the flip book to my parents," I said, and paused.

"Yeah? And what did they do that time?"

"Almost exactly the same thing. And I ran out again. But I was thinking. I didn't run into the street. The car and the taxi went past. And then an old pickup drove up onto the sidewalk and killed me. And, for my last chance, I came back farther, eight weeks, to last Monday."

"So what are you going to do this time?" he wanted to know. He seemed to be totally wrapped up in the story.

"I'm going to do the puppet show. It's a big risk, because the same thing will probably happen again. But I'm going to take that risk, because if I can't do it, then what's the point of being here anyway? I've just got to do it in a way that my parents will appreciate—so my father won't accuse me of messing around with dolls."

"That's not going to be easy—since that's just what you like to do." He laughed and walked away.

I was amazed. He hadn't hit me. Why hadn't he put more pressure on me about the English test? Was this it?

When I told Eloise on the phone, she wasn't surprised. "I thought that would be a good thing to do," she said. "You must have stood up to him better, too."

"You think he'll leave me alone now?" I asked her.

"It'll be interesting to see what he does."

"Well, thanks for saving me from getting punched out today, anyway."

"Another thing," Eloise said. "Whatever the English quiz is about, look it up, do some research. Then you'll get a better grade than last time."

The next day was the English quiz. The question was to explain the difference between a metaphor and a simile. I knew the answer, but because of what Eloise said, I looked it up to make sure and to get as many examples as possible. I had gotten a B before. This time I got an A-plus.

Somehow Meyer passed, too. He made a big deal about not getting kicked off the teams this time. But he wasn't off the hook yet. He needed to do better in all his subjects to stay on the teams.

In art class I worked on my book. It was about a man who hit a ball and then the ball never stopped. It reached escape velocity and left the gravity well of the Earth. It went up, out of the solar system, into another galaxy, and finally into orbit around a different star. Eventually life developed on the baseball. Finally an intelligent species evolved. The stitches on the baseball were towering mountain ranges to them. Flat plains stretched endlessly in between the mountain ranges. On the plains they made tremendous playing fields where they celebrated the game of baseball night and day. It was a deep religion to them.

Oddly, Kurt Meyer was fascinated by my picture book. He was making one with another kid, a girl who had a crush on him, so she didn't mind doing almost all the work as long as he flattered her and flirted with her. And then he would stroll over to my table and watch me work. "How do you know what the escape velocity of a base-ball is?" he asked me.

"I looked it up in the library," I told him. "Research." I hadn't done much research in my previous lives. This time, because Eloise had suggested it, I was doing a lot of it—I was already looking at books about marionettes, the more technical the better.

"But nobody could really hit a ball that hard, could they?" Meyer objected.

"No, they couldn't. But that's not the point. The point is to make something magical, but very realistic, too. Research helps you make it realistic. And the more realistic it is, the more you believe in the magic."

I hadn't thought about it in exactly those terms, but somehow I knew to make the book that way—Eloise had said something like that to me about how to tell the story to Meyer, and I had put it into the book without realizing it. Now that I had expressed the idea in so many words, it suddenly hit me: *That* was the solution to the puppet show. Make something magical, to express my own nature. But also make it something real, which Mom and Dad could relate to. I hadn't done it that way the first two times; I had just made it like a fantasy. Now I knew that wouldn't work with them.

As the last day of March approached, I was more helpful than ever to Mom. I was always clearing the table, washing the dishes, making my bed, telling her to sit down and I would do the work. Mom liked it. I was sure Dad didn't like seeing me do "woman's work," but he didn't humiliate me about it because he knew Mom liked the extra help.

"Better doing housework than moping around like you always did before," he said, and actually smiled.

I couldn't help smiling back. Maybe the idea I'd had up in the great white light the last time was right: My problems with Dad weren't just that *he* didn't understand *me*—the way *I* acted was part of it, too.

Mom was starting to feel a little strange and was concerned about something she didn't talk about with me, so on the last day of March she went to the doctor. Dad got home from the factory first. He was unusually nervous, pacing, not sitting down with the paper or in front of the TV. He was also watching me.

He practically jumped when he heard the front door open. "What happened?" he said, as soon as she walked through the door.

She smiled. "I'm going to have a baby."

Then they hugged each other for a while, saying things like, "It's so wonderful!" "So unbelievable!" "I didn't think this could ever happen."

Then they both turned and looked at me. I was beaming at them. "I'm so happy!" I cried, and ran over and hugged Mom. I hadn't done that the first time. "I've always wanted a little brother or sister."

"We have to tell you now, Peter," Mom said, her tone strangely hesitant. "We adopted you. We thought we couldn't have our own children, so God let us choose you."

I knew it was coming this time—I had been through this moment once before in my original life—so it didn't feel like a punch in the gut now. I didn't just mumble and run upstairs fighting tears like the first time, which had made them angry and disappointed.

"Adopted?" I said, looking blank. "Funny . . . for some reason, I'm not that surprised." I brightened. "And it makes it even *more* wonderful that now you're having your own baby."

They were looking very puzzled. "You're not that surprised about being adopted?" Dad said. "That's not what we expected. We were . . . worried about telling you." He cleared his throat and went on quickly. "And not only that. For the last couple of weeks, you've been different,

Peter. The way you've been helping your mother so much, always telling her to take it easy. Almost like you knew about that, too . . ."

I'd been hoping they would make the connection. "Well, I didn't know exactly, for sure," I said, a little shy. "But I just had this sort of feeling about it. Like maybe the most important thing I could do was to make sure Mom took it easy, so nothing would go wrong."

"But how could you know anything about it, Peter?" Mom said—because of growing up on a farm, she was always very practical. "*I* didn't even have any idea until less than a week ago."

"I don't know how I knew." I shrugged. "I just had this feeling that something might be happening. And, most of all, I wanted to be sure there wouldn't be any problems."

They turned and looked at each other, then back to me. Dad shook his head, smiling. "I never expected anything like this from you, Peter."

My reaction this time to the news about being adopted, and Mom having a new baby, was completely different from the first time. This might be the biggest change of all. Maybe I was really on the right track now.

Dad was shaking his head. "Almost like you knew. Looks like we have a psychotic on our hands, Peter."

"Psychic." I couldn't help correcting him.

His smile disappeared—he didn't like being corrected by me. He turned quickly back to Mom. "I'll take your coat, dear. Sit down, sit down. Peter!" he ordered me. "Get your mother some . . . something. . . ."

"Coming right up." I hurried into the kitchen and brought out the tray of milk and graham crackers I'd prepared. I put it down on the coffee table in front of Mom. "Don't worry about supper, Mom. I'm making hot dogs and beans. It's all ready, just needs to be warmed up."

Dad was shaking his head, staring at me.

I began to build the puppet stage much earlier than before—not in shop class at school, but at home, in the basement. And soon after that, the real trouble started.

<<eleven

<<Dad had alternate Saturdays off, and a week later, I asked him if he could take me to the lumberyard.

"Lumberyard? What do *you* want to go there for?"

"I want to build something. I planned it out. I know just what I need to buy. I've been saving the money."

"What do you want to build?"

I couldn't tell him yet. If he knew it was for a puppet stage, he probably wouldn't take me. Once he saw how good I was at sawing and hammering nails and other things that he thought boys should like, then maybe he would be more likely to accept the fact that it was a puppet stage.

"It's something for the baby," was what I said.

He lifted his eyebrows but didn't ask me any more questions about it. What I said was true, in a way—I would love to entertain the baby with puppet shows.

I had just barely enough money for the wood and other stuff I needed. Of course, Dad didn't offer to help pay. He was always telling me I was lucky I got an allowance and didn't have to have a job. When we loaded the stuff into the car, I carried a lot so he would see I wasn't a weakling.

I started building it that day. I used a design from one of the books about puppeteering that I had found at the library. This stage was going to be a lot more elaborate than the one I had made before. Behind and above the stage was a platform called a bridge that the puppeteer stood on. A ladder with four flat steps led up to it. The bridge had a railing in front of it, for the puppeteer to lean on, to help him support the puppets. It also had lots and lots of hooks, for holding the puppets onstage as well as offstage.

Dad would come down to the basement sometimes to see what I was doing. "That's not the way to hold a saw," he said. "You're jerking it. You need to pull some weight into it, like this."

He liked it that I let him act like he was an expert, and he enjoyed showing off what he knew. And, for

once—since he didn't know it was a puppet stage yet—
I was doing something he approved of. For a while we
were getting along better than I ever remembered. I was
beginning to hope.

And both Dad and I were being very good to Mom.
Making her life easy and comfortable was an activity we
shared—I washed the dishes often now, and sometimes
Dad and I did it together and talked.

One day after school Mom said to me, "It's . . . not
easy for me to talk about these kinds of things, Peter."
She kept her eyes on her knitting. "But I know your father can be hard on you sometimes—it's his way. I'm glad
you two are getting along so much better now." Her
knitting picked up speed. "You better go unload the dish-
washer."

She had never said anything like that to me before.

Miss Lilly gushed over my picture book. She liked it a
lot better than the haunted house one I had made in my
original life. I knew this one was better because I had
done research, and it was realistic as well as fantastic.

It was Friday, April 13, the day we finished the picture books. I was nervous about showing mine to Mom
and Dad. They were bored when I showed the first picture book to them on this Friday in my original life. And
they had forgotten about it when the news came on
about the fire at Robinson's Department Store, where so
many people had died.

When I got home, Mom was getting ready to go out. "Could you make supper tonight, Peter?" she said. "Put the chicken in a 350-degree oven at five o'clock." She sounded companionable, not curt and practical like she had always been in my other lives.

"Sure, that's easy. Where are you going?"

"Today's the last day of a big sale on baby stuff at Robinson's," she said. "I never would have known about it if you hadn't washed the dishes last night. I had time to look at the whole paper; I never used to. When you do the chicken, don't forget . . ."

But that's where the fire was today. I couldn't let Mom go! I didn't think first about a clever way to stop her, I just said, "Mom, you can't go to Robinson's."

"What are you talking about?"

"Just . . . don't go to Robinson's."

"Why on earth not?" She sounded surprised.

She wouldn't have known about the sale if I hadn't washed the dishes last night—that was a change I had made from my original life. Could I tell her there was going to be a fire at Robinson's, and a lot of people would die? But what proof did I have? She'd probably just get mad at me and go anyway. And whatever happened, then she and Dad would know I knew about the fire in advance. That would make problems.

"Uh . . . I don't feel very good," I said.

She felt my forehead. "No fever," she said.

"I feel like I'm getting a cold."

"You're eleven years old. You can take care of yourself for a few hours. We have aspirin and decongestant. Here I was thinking you were getting over being so babyish."

Now I really *did* feel sick. I sank into a chair, feeling the blood drain from my face. "I don't know what's wrong with me, I just feel terrible, my stomach, too."

"This came on pretty sudden," she said, sitting down across from me. "A minute ago you were all happy and eager to make supper. Now you can hardly stand up." She was studying me closely. "You do look pretty pale."

"There'll be other sales," I mumbled.

"You better lie down in bed," she said gruffly, not pleased. But now I could tell she wasn't going to go. "I'll take your temperature, just to be sure, and bring you some aspirin and hot lemonade with honey." She sighed. "I was really excited about that sale."

I got in bed, still feeling terrible. I was worrying about the people who were going to die in the fire. I had to try to save them. Why hadn't I thought about this before? I waited until Mom finished with me.

When I heard the TV go on downstairs, I snuck into Mom and Dad's room, where the upstairs phone was. I remembered the fire had started in the appliance department, a faulty electrical connection in a display stove. I got the number for the appliance department, and when the man answered, I told him he should check the wiring on the stoves—I said I'd been there earlier and noticed a burning smell.

"Why didn't you say something about it then?" he wanted to know, as if he didn't believe me.

"I . . . I was distracted. But it was pretty strong. You better check on it or a lot of people could get hurt."

"Is this a practical joke? You sound like a kid."

What could I say? "*You* might die if you don't do something about it," I said, hoping he would believe me.

After Dad got home, I came downstairs and lay on the couch. I was nervous about the fire and had to see what was going to happen on the news.

Dad was sitting in his chair, watching TV; Mom was in the kitchen. "So your mother says there's something wrong with you. She couldn't go to her sale because you felt too sick to stay home alone." He said it very disapprovingly.

"Yeah," I said weakly. "And I still feel—"

"Shh! Wait a minute," he said, waving his hand to shush me. He leaned forward, staring hard at the TV. There were fire engines outside of Robinson's.

". . . An anonymous phone call prevented what could have been the worst fire in the metropolitan area in years," the newscaster was saying. "Because of the call, there were only a few injuries and no deaths."

I felt like jumping up and down and shouting for joy.

But I was supposed to be sick. And I wasn't supposed to know about the fire ahead of time.

"Gert! Come in here, right away!" Dad called out. "Where was that sale you wanted to go to today?"

She came into the living room, wiping her hands on her apron. "What's the matter? That sale was at Robinson's. Why are you—" Then she saw the picture of the fire engines in front of Robinson's on the TV, and her mouth fell open.

"The fire department is asking the caller to identify himself so he can be rewarded," the announcer was saying. "The voice sounded like a very young teenage boy."

They watched until the story was over and the commercial came on. Then Dad switched off the TV. They both turned and stared at me.

"You started treating your mother differently before we knew she was going to have a baby," Dad said slowly. "You didn't seem surprised about being adopted. And now this. Are you really psychotic, or what?"

This time I knew better than to correct him.

"Were you really sick today?" Dad asked. "Are you saying it was all a coincidence?"

"What else could it be?" I said shakily.

Now Mom looked pale. "I would have been there if you hadn't said you were sick," she said, her voice rising. "You didn't want me to go to Robinson's. I felt it." She was remembering now. "You didn't start feeling sick until *after* you found out where I was going. You knew there might be a fire there today, just like you knew I was pregnant. How did you know? Are you the one who made the phone call?"

"No. It was a coincidence. I just felt sick." Their case was pretty strong. It was probably pointless to argue. I was just afraid I'd get in worse trouble if they found out I knew what was going to happen in the next four weeks.

"You're lying!" Dad accused me. "You know things ahead. There's something you're not telling us."

"I don't know things. I have feelings," I said. "And now I feel sick, okay? And why are you mad at me, anyway? Do you wish Mom had gone to Robinson's?" I pushed myself up from the sofa and ran upstairs.

Of course, I was glad I had prevented the fire—last time twenty-five people had died, and this time I had saved their lives. But I couldn't tell that to Mom and Dad, and now Dad was really mad at me for talking back. I was acting like a baby again. Would I ever learn to think first? If I didn't, it probably wouldn't matter what else I did; I'd die anyway.

I'd been doing pretty well, until today.

When they accused me of lying, I should have stayed calm and confident. How could I ever do that?

I didn't go downstairs all evening. Eventually Mom brought me up a bowl of canned chicken soup and some crackers. But Dad stayed mad at me. He didn't talk to me for the rest of the weekend.

Eloise phoned on Saturday—luckily, Mom and Dad were out. "Peter, are you the one who made the anonymous phone call about that fire?" she asked me.

"Yes," I said proudly.

"Why did you wait until the last minute?" she said almost angrily. "You knew about it almost four weeks ahead. Think of those people who were injured."

She wasn't proud of me? "But last time twenty-five people died!" I said. "I saved their lives!"

"That's great, that's better than not doing anything. But we can't let anything else get this close to happening again. You've got to remember things. You have to do more good with this knowledge you have."

"Isn't saving their lives—and my life—enough?" I asked her.

"No," she said. "See you on Monday."

<<TWELVE

<<**IT WAS WARMER** now; there were tiny leaves on the trees. But I still felt terrible.

"Our new project is to make papier-mâché marionettes," Miss Lilly announced on Monday.

Kurt Meyer, at the table next to me, groaned.

This time I didn't groan. I had already done sketches of my puppets. I couldn't let anybody see them—then they would get the idea I knew about the project ahead of time.

Miss Lilly talked about papier-mâché for a while and told the class to get to work on their sketches. When we were all busy, she stepped outside.

Meyer came right over. "Did you know about that fire?" he whispered, his eyes like slits.

He wouldn't believe me if I said I forgot—it was big news. "Yeah," I said. "And my Mom almost went. I had to pretend I was sick, and then call the store and warn them."

"A little late," he said slowly. "My mother and my little brother *did* go to Robinson's on Friday."

"What!" I said, so loud that other kids turned and looked. I dropped my voice. "But . . . are they . . ."

"They got out in time, barely. They weren't hurt," Meyer said. "But they could have been. It would have been nice of you to warn me about it. I mean, since I already knew about your little secret anyway. And you knew about the fire four weeks ahead of time."

"But how could I know they were going? Did they go last time? You didn't say anything about it, and we were working every day on the—"

"There wasn't any last time for me, dope."

"Get to work, Kurt!" Miss Lilly said, coming back into the room.

"Those sketches on your table weren't the puppets you told me you made before," Meyer said to me after class. "Were you lying? You better tell me. You owe me big."

"I'm doing a different puppet show. If I do something different, maybe my folks will like it; maybe they won't get mad, and maybe I won't die. Okay?"

"Not really," he said. We were out in the hall now. "I liked that flip book thing you said we did last time. Especially because I could boss you around and not have to do any work and not have to make a dumb puppet myself."

He was mad at me because I hadn't warned him about the fire. "But I told you, I have to make the puppet show."

Eloise approached us. "You stay out of this," Meyer said, though she hadn't said a word.

Now I was angry as well as scared. "She's only about a hundred times smarter than you," I said pointlessly.

"The two of you together can't beat me," he said. "I'm telling you, I don't want to make a stupid puppet; I want to make a flip book with you. I know Lilly will let us do that because you said it happened before. In the next art class, on Wednesday, you'll tell her you want to make a flip book with me." He stopped walking and stood in front of me so I couldn't move. "And if you don't go along with it, then I'll tell Robinson's and the fire department that you knew about the fire for four weeks and didn't do anything until the last minute. It's your fault those people got hurt." He turned and walked away.

"Can you change the past and fix it so a cement block falls on his head?" Eloise said.

"I've got to do something," I said, clutching my books. "I have to make those puppets. And he can't tell them I knew about the fire. Help me think of what to do, Eloise. I'm depending on you. Meet me after school."

"We also have to talk about what I was saying on Saturday—other ways you might be able to help people because of what you know about the future."

For the rest of the school day, I thought about Meyer telling them I knew about the fire way ahead. They wouldn't think I was a hero for making the call; they would think I was careless and selfish for waiting until the last minute. Mom and Dad would think it was my fault, too. It would turn them against me.

But how could I stop Meyer? I was so nervous now, I couldn't think clearly. If Eloise couldn't come up with an idea, I'd be sunk.

"Maybe the problem with Meyer, and the problem with how to help people with what you know, can go together," she said on the way home. "Think back. Think really hard. What happened? Anything else big like the fire?"

I tried to concentrate. "No. Nothing like that."

"That's good. Okay, how about smaller things? Even if it seems unimportant, it might help."

I tried to concentrate. "Well, Dad got real upset because he forgot to change the oil, and then he had to pay a lot of money to get the car fixed."

"That's something. You can help him with that."

"But then they'll know I know what's going to happen!"

"We'll deal with that later. Anything else?"

"Well . . ." And then I remembered. Suddenly I was excited, not so worried. "Meyer got grounded for a month because he pushed his little brother too hard on a swing and he fell off and broke his shoulder."

"Oh, wow," Eloise breathed. "That's a *great* one. It'll be easy to figure out how to use that. What else?"

"You want to know what happens to you?" I asked her.

"If there's something really disastrous I could avoid, tell me. Otherwise, I don't want to know."

That was typical of her. "No disasters," I said, and felt good enough to smile at her.

"How about more general things, like stuff from the local news or the local section of the paper?" Eloise asked me.

"Hmmmm." I had been so preoccupied with my artwork during my previous lives that I hadn't paid much attention to the news. But I did remember that the mayor had a stroke in Canada at the beginning of May and died while they were trying to get him home. His doctor said if he'd had a checkup before going, he'd probably still be alive.

She asked me a few more questions about it. I told her the details I remembered. Then she said, "An anonymous letter can save the mayor. I'll write it on my computer."

"All right, an anonymous letter will save the mayor," I said. "But how do I tell Dad about the car? Then they'll *know* I can see the future."

She shrugged. "So?"

"But . . . they can't find out about me dying and coming back to life. That would ruin everything for sure."

"They don't have to know that. Just tell them you get these last-minute insights, or something. Be vague. It seems to me that if you help them, they'll be glad and won't wonder exactly how you do it."

I thought about that. "You know, they were impressed that I had this feeling I should be helping Mom before they knew she was pregnant. They got mad about the fire, but that was because I wouldn't admit I knew about it."

"Well, admit it now." She paused, and then spoke a little more gently. "Just be cool and straightforward about it. Don't mumble, Peter." Then she went on more quickly again. "And keep thinking about other things that are going to happen. The more stuff you come up with, the better. Help your dad about the car. And it'll be a piece of cake to use what you know about Meyer's little brother to get him off your back. Call me if you think of anything else."

"Listen," I said that night at dinner. "I wasn't sick on Friday. You were right. I did know Mom should stay away from Robinson's, but I didn't want to admit it. I made the anonymous phone call, but I don't want anybody to know because I don't want that kind of attention."

They looked at each other, then at me. For some reason, Dad didn't seem angry, as he had been all weekend. "How did you know?" he asked.

"Hard to explain," I said, trying not to be meek. "Sometimes I just get these special feelings, strong but vague, like the feeling that I should be making things easier for Mom. And the feeling she shouldn't go to Robinson's. And the feeling you better get the oil changed, Dad. If you don't do it right away, it'll be bad for the car, and you might have to pay a lot of money to fix it."

He slapped his forehead. "You're right! It's way overdue, and I keep forgetting. How did you . . ." He paused. "It was one of your special feelings, right? So far these feelings have been pretty helpful. I'll take care of it tomorrow."

Eloise had been right. He didn't press me to tell him how I knew. And he wasn't mad at me anymore.

The next day, Tuesday, I talked to Eloise first, then went up to Meyer after gym class.

"Listen, Meyer, I can help you big if you lay off about the flip book and telling that I knew about the fire."

"You're acting pretty sure of yourself," he said skeptically. "Help me how?"

"I happen to know you're going to get in big trouble because of something you do next Sunday. Your parents are going to ground you for a month. I'll tell you how to prevent it, if you forget about the flip book."

He looked hard at me. He didn't like letting me have the upper hand. "How can I be sure?"

"I knew about the game. I knew about the fire. I know about this."

"Then why can't you help me by telling me what's going to be on the English test?" he wanted to know.

"Because I don't remember. Do *you* remember test questions a month later?"

He couldn't argue with that. "Well . . ."

He still wasn't buying it. I had to make him a better offer. "Plus, I'll help you with your puppet," I said rashly. "I can use the puppet we make in my show, if you do it the way I want. It'll help me and you, too."

"First tell me what—"

"No. First, *you* agree to make the puppet. Then I'll tell you what I know, *after* art class on Wednesday."

He glared at me with open hostility. He hated letting me be in control. "We'll see," he said. "And if what you tell me isn't good enough, I'll still tell about the fire." He turned and stomped away.

Eloise had been wrong about one thing. Meyer wasn't going to be a piece of cake.

<<Thirteen

<<Tuesday night, Dad came home from work chuckling. "I took the car to the mechanic at lunchtime," he said. "Everything was fine, but he told me if I'd waited a couple more days to get the oil changed, I would have had hundreds of dollars of repairs." He beamed at me and slapped me on the back. "Be sure to tell us about any more of these feelings you have, Pete. They're real helpful."

I was so happy using what I knew to help Mom and Dad, not to mention get them on my side. Eloise had been right.

But Meyer could still wreck everything.

So now I had to help him with his puppet, along with

everything else I had to do in three and a half wee
had already been planning to make three puppets instea
of two, for the show I wanted to do. How was I going to
find time to help Meyer with a fourth one?

But the first problem was how to do it in a way Miss
Lilly would approve of. I told Meyer before art on Wednesday that we had to ask her together—and the more
enthusiastic he seemed, the more willing she would be.

"I have to act enthusiastic about puppets?" he said,
grimacing. "What if some of the guys hear me?"

"I'm just telling you—you groan every time she an-
nounces a new project. If you act like you're interested
for a change, she might let me help you."

He sighed. "I'm not going to say it very loud."

I explained to Miss Lilly that I was planning a big
puppet show, and I didn't have time to make four puppets, and Kurt would help me—he liked this project,
after all.

Miss Lilly and I looked at him.

His eyes shifted from side to side. "Yeah, I thought
this puppet stuff was dumb, at first," he said, talking very
quietly. "But then I saw what Pete was sketching and . . ."
It was all he could do not to turn around and see if anybody was listening. "I began to think it was pretty cool.
But I'm clumsy about stuff like this. So, if Pete helps
me a little, he can use the puppet I make in his show."

really going on here?" Miss Lilly said suspi-
... never expected to see you two working to-
... mean, Peter's always so clever and enthusiastic,
...urt ... Well, anyway, I'm surprised."

"It would really help me a lot, Miss Lilly," I said,
since I knew Meyer didn't want to say any more.

"For you, Peter, okay," she said. She turned to Meyer.
"I'll have my eyes on you. If you want a good grade,
you've got to work, too. I don't want Peter doing it all."

Back at the table, his face hardened. "Okay. What's
this information you have that's going to help me so
much? If it's not good, I'm telling about the fire."

"Next Sunday you're going to be pushing your little
brother on a swing. He's going to fall off and break his
shoulder. Your parents are going to blame you for it.
They're going to ground you for a month."

"I'd never take my brother to the swings!" he said
sharply. "For this, you roped me into making a puppet?"

I felt like sighing, but suppressed the impulse—I was
beginning to see that sighing a lot didn't have a great
effect on other people. "It happened last time. And if
you know what's good for you, you'll be careful."

"We'll see," he said. "So what's this puppet I'm supposed to make for your show? Not one of those ones you
were sketching. Too much work."

What kind of puppet could Meyer make?

And then the most brilliant idea I'd had yet for the new show just popped into my head. I probably never would have thought of it if I weren't working with Meyer. I quickly sketched it, keeping it really simple.

"Yeah, that looks easier than the others," he said.

"Start with the body," I told him. "That's the easiest part."

So I worked on three puppets, and Meyer clumsily began molding the fourth one. I had to help him a lot at first. But when he started catching on and getting better, I began to hope that I might begin to save time with Meyer's help.

Meanwhile, Dad had actually admired the puppet stage when he came down to look at it on the day he took the car in. I explained about the bridge, the railing, the hooks.

"This is good solid work, Pete," he said. His face tightened a little. "But this puppet stuff is kinda sissy. If you were building something real, like a go-cart..." He shook his head, as if trying to shake away his disappointment in me. "Anyway, it's still a good job."

I tried not to beam with pleasure.

"Waste of time," Mom said when we went back upstairs, not looking up from her knitting, the needles clicking away. It was really tough to get past the farm girl in her.

"Sure, it's a waste of time," Dad said. "But he's doing a good sturdy job of wasting his time."

"You think the baby might like puppet shows?" I said. "It's kind of a present for him—or her."

Mom softened a little. "Well, for the baby . . ."

"I'll get you some hot milk," I said, and retreated into the kitchen. When I came back, they were absorbed by the TV again, no longer talking about me, to my relief.

On Friday, I warned Meyer, "Be careful on Sunday."

"I never take my brother to the park," he stated flatly. "And when it doesn't happen, you've had it."

I worried about it over the weekend, working on the stage. Would Meyer take his brother to the park? If he did, would he push him hard enough to break his shoulder? If Meyer was nasty enough to do that, on purpose, when he knew about it ahead of time, then I couldn't trust him about anything.

"So what happened?" I asked him on Monday.

"You're really worried about the little brat?" he said, shaking his head and grinning. "I thought you were getting tougher, Pete, but you're still a softy underneath."

Again, I stifled the urge to sigh. "Okay, forget it." I was worried about his little brother. But I had also been hoping I might be able to get him over to the house for the puppet show, in hopes of impressing Dad. "Just tell me: Did they ground you or not?"

"It was real interesting," he said, more serious now. "I tested what you told me. I didn't do anything unusual, like offer to take him to the park. I just waited to see what would happen. And on Sunday, he starts begging to go, and Mom and Dad are both working in their garden, and they ask me to do it." Now he was talking to me as if I were one of his friends. "And I didn't have anything else to do, a game or anything. It was all happening like you said. So I went along with it. We go to the park. He's all excited about going with *me*. And we went to the swings." He paused.

"Yeah? Go on," I urged him. I couldn't help it.

"Well, I would have been angry about taking him to the park, if I didn't know about it first. So I was careful. I didn't push hard. He didn't fall." He lifted his arms. "And I didn't get grounded. You got any other tips for me?"

"If I remember anything else, I'll tell you," I said. "Except I don't remember any—"

"Test questions," he finished for me. "Maybe I still don't believe that. But I won't tell about the fire, yet."

Meyer was working on the smallest, simplest puppet. I had thought that would be the easiest one for him to make, but now he was having problems. His big fat fingers were good at throwing and catching balls, but lousy at making small features. And even though this puppet was the smallest and simplest, it was also, in a very real way, the most important. It had to be done beautifully.

I designed it so the feet were invisible, but not the tiny hands. "Uh . . . you need to do the hands over again another time," I told Meyer, when he presented me with the second version of them. It wasn't easy for me to tell him what to do, but at the same time I enjoyed being the boss on this project instead of the other way around, like last time. "These hands are too blobby, like monster's hands."

He scowled. "It's boring doing the same thing over and over again."

"I thought you wanted her to give you a good grade," I said. "If you make something sloppy, she won't do that."

"All right, all right, I'll do the stupid things again," he muttered, and stomped back to his table.

That night I took time off from working on the stage and made pairs of tiny hands. I had to make several versions of each hand until I got two that were right. The next day I brought them to school in my shirt pocket.

In art, I stood behind Meyer. "Here," I whispered. I pointed my finger, as if instructing him, and let the hands I had made fall out of my fist onto the table.

"Great," he whispered back. "Now I can move on to some other *wonderful* part of this dumb project."

The head was a lot more difficult than the hands. This part I couldn't cheat and make myself—Miss Lilly would be able to tell. Anyway, I was behind schedule with the three puppets I was making, and with the stage, too.

And Meyer botched the head once, twice, three times. "I know you can do it," I encouraged him. "It's different from sports. You have to be really slow and delicate."

"Maybe I don't feel like being really slow and delicate," he said, mimicking the way I said it.

"Do you feel like staying on the teams?"

"Shut up and let me work."

Every night I washed all the dishes, which took a lot of time. But it was important to keep on helping Mom. I cooked several times a week. That meant I had to stay up later and later to paint the stage, to get it done in time. And now Mom never seemed to notice how much I was helping.

One day Mom came down to the basement when I was working on the stage. I expected her to tell me it was a waste of time, that I should be outside or studying math, and how I was darker around the eyes than ever. But she said, very hesitantly, "Peter, I'd like to ask you something."

"Sure," I said, putting down the hammer. "What is it?"

She wouldn't meet my eye; whatever she was going to say wasn't easy for her. "Well, these feelings you have, about what's going to happen . . ."

"Yes?" I said, suddenly scared.

She looked at me. "The baby?" she said. "Is the baby going to be all right?" She looked down again.

I didn't know. I only knew what was going to happen until May 11, a little over a week from now, the night I died. I didn't know what to say.

"You knew I was going to have the baby before I did," she prodded me. "You knew about the fire. You knew about the car. So what about . . ." She couldn't bring herself to say it again.

"I don't know things very far ahead," I said, trying to sound sure of myself. "But I'm sure everything's okay."

"You better stop that hammering the minute your father gets home. The racket drives him crazy." She turned and went upstairs.

She was angry that I hadn't answered her question. Now I felt self-conscious about every sound I made. She was more negative about me and the puppets than ever.

That night Dad came down when I was doing some quiet work on the stage. Without a word he picked up the hammer and started finishing a place I had put aside until he wasn't home. "I thought you didn't like the noise at night," I couldn't keep from saying.

He didn't say anything; he just kept on hammering.

I didn't express my shock and happiness. I went on working along with him, in companionable silence.

It lasted less than five minutes. "Frank, what on earth are you doing?" Mom said from the stairs.

He looked up at her with a guilty expression, nails in his mouth.

"You know I can't stand that noise in the evenings. It disturbs me."

He instantly put down the hammer and took the nails out of his mouth. "Oh, sorry, Gert," he said, sounding very bashful. "I'm really sorry. I wasn't thinking. I just saw Pete working so hard, and thought maybe I could—"

"No, you weren't thinking, were you? About me and my condition."

Dad hurried up the stairs and put one hand around her waist and the other on her elbow. "Come on up, Gert. Not too fast." He turned back to me. "Peter, stop that nonsense right away and come and get her some warm milk and crackers," he said angrily. "On the double. You're acting like that stupid stage is more important than your mother. I don't want you working on it any-more."

They already hated it, and I hadn't even done the show.

"I'm sorry, Peter. I goofed," Eloise apologized the next day at school. She seemed afraid to meet my eye. That was ominous.

"I was so excited about the letter, and all the research I did in medical books, that I didn't think," she said. "I must have put it in one of the envelopes with our return address on the back. I didn't double-check. They called yesterday."

"Eloise, what are you talking about?" I said.

She clenched her fists in frustration. "The anonymous letter to the mayor!" she said. "The letter telling him he has amaurosis fugax—that it wasn't just a little eye problem, it was a transient ischemic attack, and if he doesn't go to the doctor right away, he'll have a really bad stroke in Canada."

It finally sank in. "You warned him about what was going to happen—and they traced it back to you?"

She nodded miserably, still not looking at me.

"What did they say?" I asked her, feeling cold.

"They want to make a big deal about it. Publicity. They want to honor the person who saved the mayor's life—the person who can see the future. I acted dumb; I didn't tell them exactly who can see the future, but they're not going to leave us alone. They said they were going to tell the press about it today."

This was the worst. Eloise didn't have to spell it out for me. If the world believed I could see the future, I would be followed, hounded. Everybody would want to know what was going to happen to the world, and to themselves.

And a lot of the people coming at me would be crazy.

<<Fourteen

<<It was Friday, May 4, one week before I had died the other times. I was getting more nervous about that as the day got closer. "We have to keep them away until after the show," I said. "If they find out it's me before that—then everything will go wrong. Mom and Dad will never learn to appreciate me, never. I'll probably do something crazy again and get killed for the last time."

"I can't *believe* I was so stupid!" Eloise said.

"What are we going to do?"

The bell rang. I went to Meyer's table.

Meyer had just about gotten the head right, amazingly. But he still had to make another one, with bigger eyes. He didn't want to. We had argued about it at the end of art class on Wednesday. I expected him to be sullen today.

"Don't be so edgy, Pete," he said. "Be happy you're going to be honored by the mayor."

I turned on him. *"What?"*

"I heard what she told you." He held up the puppet head so Miss Lilly would think we were discussing it.

"Don't make any threats," I muttered.

"Now why would you think I'd make a threat?" he said, grinning. "I'm talking about a deal. If I don't have to do this head again, I promise not to lead them to you today."

I was so disgusted with him for taking advantage of the terrible situation I was in that suddenly I wasn't even scared of what he would do. I walked over to my puppets and opened up the paint box and got to work.

I painted the puppet and tried to figure out how to keep myself hidden from the mayor's office and the press. What if Eloise said she was the one who knew the future? But then *she'd* be in danger from crackpots.

"Uh, Pete?" Meyer said.

I didn't answer or look up; I went on calmly working.

"What I said about leading them to you—that was a joke. Okay? Uh . . . you really don't care if I make the head over again?" He sounded almost disappointed.

"It's not my problem if you get kicked off the teams."

He started to say something, then thought better of it. He began working on a new head—with bigger eyes.

"I'll tell them it's me who can see the future," Eloise said unhappily in the hallway after class. "I'll get the attention, and you'll be able to do the show."

"But then *you'll* be the target of all the crazies!" I said. "You won't be safe. You'll have to go into hiding."

"Hey, you two, wait up," Meyer called from behind us.

"We're busy," I said. We kept walking.

He pushed past some kids and walked beside us. "I know what you're worried about. All the attention will interfere with your show. Maybe I could help."

We didn't say anything.

"I know you two think I'm stupid, but I'm good at some things. You need me to help you with this."

Eloise and I glanced at each other. She must have been thinking what I was—he really seemed to want to help.

"You saved the mayor's life, but you have to hide from all the publicity—that's pretty exciting," he said, his eyes glowing. "I want to be part of it. And I have an idea. Somebody gets the attention away from you."

"Who?" I said, wondering what he was getting at.

"Me," he announced, beaming.

"Huh?" Eloise and I both said.

"It's so simple," he said. "I just say *I'm* the one who can see the future. They don't know who it is, right?"

"Right," said Eloise.

"And you guys back me up. And then I'll get all the attention you don't want, so you can do what you have to do. Plus, I'll get to be in the paper and maybe on TV."

"But aren't you worried about—" I started to say.

"What a great idea, Kurt!" Eloise interrupted me, shooting me a steely look. "How generous and thoughtful of you! I'll be glad to back you up that you're the one who can see the future." She reached out her hand.

"Deal," Meyer said, beaming, shaking her hand up and down, and then mine. "When are you going to tell them?"

"As soon as school is over. Maybe you should come home with me. There might already be reporters there."

"Sure," Meyer said, lifting his chin like a true hero.

He had no idea what he was getting into.

"But don't forget, you have to finish that head," I said. "The one I saw you making today looked really good."

"Okay, okay," he said, still focused on Eloise.

That night we watched Meyer and Eloise on the local news. It was a warm night, but Meyer wore his heavy letter jacket. They stood on a lawn in front of the mayor's mansion. The mayor shook their hands. "I wouldn't be here today if it weren't for this young man," he said. He presented Meyer with some kind of medal.

After the ceremony, reporters held microphones up to him. "How did you know the mayor was sick, and what was wrong with him?" they asked him.

"Sometimes I just get these feelings," Meyer said, sounding a little bashful. It was just what Eloise had told me to say; she had coached him. "I don't know when they're going to come, and I don't know everything that's going to happen. I just knew the mayor would die in Canada if he didn't go to his doctor first."

They turned to Eloise. "But you wrote the letter?"

"I knew Kurt had this ability," she said, very poised. "I asked him to think hard, if there was any good he could do." She wasn't above taking some of the credit, I was glad to see. "He knew about the mayor, and I wrote the letter."

Back to Meyer. "So, what about the big game tomorrow?" a reporter asked, smiling.

Meyer shook his head. "Don't know. The future just comes to me every once in a while. I can't predict when."

"Well, Kurt Meyer, you've already done one very good deed. We look forward to more." The segment ended.

Mom and Dad were confused. "What is this, something going around?" Dad asked me. "You know those kids?"

"They're my two best friends," I said.

"That big guy's your friend? But he's wearing a letter jacket!"

I shrugged. "He's working on my project with me, the show I'm going to do."

"That guy?" Dad said, shaking his head. "Working on your project? Huh!"

"But does he have the same kind of feelings you do, about what's going to happen?" Mom wanted to know.

"Eloise wrote that letter. But I'm the one who knew the mayor would die if he didn't go to the doctor. Meyer doesn't know a thing about the future."

"But then why is he up there getting all the credit instead of you?" Dad demanded.

"He's doing me a favor," I said.

"A *favor*? To take all the attention from you?"

"Wait and see what happens," I said.

Mom was watching me in a funny way over her knitting, smiling a little—almost as though she was proud of me.

<<fifteen

<<there was a story about Meyer in the Sunday paper. It focused on the incident with the mayor but also said he had made the anonymous phone call to Robinson's—he hadn't known about the fire until the last minute. The article said he was a great athlete. The picture was flattering. I wondered if he would have a chance to enjoy it at all.

Meyer looked tired and pale when he came into art class on Monday. "What's happening?" Eloise asked him.

His grin was a little lopsided. "Everything's great," he said. "I've never been so popular. We're getting an unlisted number."

"The attention—it's fun?" I asked him.

"Sure! Why shouldn't it—" Then he saw the way Eloise

and I were watching him. "Well, some of it is. But some of it isn't," he admitted. And then the other kids surrounded him, and we got pushed out of the way. Miss Lilly had to yell twice to get them to settle down.

The head that Meyer had started on Friday was one I could really use. It wasn't as good as I would have done, but it was good enough. He had two more days in art class to put the puppet together and rig it. But that was the easy part. My puppets were almost done.

After class Meyer told the other kids to lay off, and he walked with me. "You remember anything else, Pete?" he asked me, a little desperately. "Anything that happened in the next few days? It would help me if I could just come up with something else for these people."

"All I can remember is the show," I said truthfully. "If I can think of anything, I'll let you know right away."

"You better. This is a favor to you, you know," he said grimly. He told me their new unlisted number.

I couldn't think of anything, so I didn't call. On Tuesday, there was a segment on the news showing a large crowd of people outside Meyer's house, and police keeping them at a safe distance. "So *that's* why you let him take the credit," Dad said. "Pretty smart."

Meyer didn't show up at school on Wednesday. It looked as if I was going to have to rig his puppet myself.

"I wonder how he's dealing with this," Eloise said after school. "I'm almost kind of worried about him."

"Yeah," I said. "I have his new number."

I called from a pay phone. Meyer didn't answer, of course. As soon as I asked for him, his mother hung up.

Eloise tried. "Hello, this is Eloise, Kurt's friend from school who was on TV with him," she said quickly. His mother got him. Eloise handed me the receiver.

"It's me, Pete," I said. "How come you weren't in—"

"I can't handle this!" he said. He was breathing hard. "I'm telling them it was you all along. I'll call the mayor. I have to! I can't—"

"Don't do anything crazy. Just tell me about it."

"The reporters are bad enough, but the others are worse. Crazies! They can't phone anymore, but they keep coming to the house. They followed me to school on Monday and waited for me all day and came back with me. Sick people, poor people, all kinds of cases begging me to help them. They ask me about future obituaries. I can't go outside. There are cops around the house to keep them away. But they're always out there waiting. I think I've got to tell the mayor it was you."

"Just wait until Saturday. After the puppet show. It'll ruin everything if it happens before then."

"You can't make me wait."

"But it was your idea to do this!"

"I don't care." He hung up.

I felt so weak I had to lean against the phone booth. "The crazies won't leave him alone," I told Eloise. "He's going to tell the mayor it was me."

"Tell him to say it was me," Eloise said bravely. "It won't make any difference to him, and then you'll be safe."

"But *you* won't be!"

"But I won't *die*, like you might."

I called him back. I said who I was, and his mother hung up on me.

"He won't talk to us anymore," I said. "We can't get near the house. He's going to tell them it was me! It could happen at any minute. What am I going to do?"

"He doesn't have to tell them it was anybody, now that I think about it," she said. "All he has to say is that he was covering for a friend who wanted to be anonymous. If he thought of that, you'd be fine."

I groaned. "But there's no way for us to tell him that! Will he think of it?"

Eloise looked away. "I'd be surprised if he did. Uh . . . maybe we should put up a roadblock on your street, so there won't be *any* cars going by after the show."

"Thanks," I said, though her idea only made me feel worse. "I think I have to do it without a roadblock."

On Friday, Miss Lilly approved Kurt's puppet—he would get her recommendation whenever he came back to school. Since he wasn't back in school, I hoped that meant he hadn't told them it was me who could see the future—yet.

I packed up the puppets and worried. I knew that the whole idea of the puppet show still disgusted Mom and Dad. It was a painful example of everything that was wrong about me.

And what if crazy people started calling us and ringing our doorbell? Whatever happened then, it would prevent Mom and Dad from understanding that it was a good thing for me to be an artist.

I set everything up carefully. The stage wasn't completely finished, but it would do. I even had a chance to practice the show for real, manipulating the controls, hanging the puppets on their hooks when working with the other ones, trying out different voices in an undertone. I kept waiting for the phone or doorbell to ring.

I approached Mom and Dad after dinner, sitting in the living room. Maybe I was getting along with them a little better this time, but in another way, this was worse than the other times, because then they were not already against what I was doing in the basement, like they were now. "Mom and Dad, I want you to see something," I said, trying to sound casual, hoping my voice wasn't shaking. "It's downstairs."

They looked up at me from the TV. "We know what's in the basement," Dad said.

"You'd be better off studying math," Mom said.

"But you have to watch the show," I urged them, trying not to sound panicky. "It's really important. I've been working so hard because I wanted to do something for you—and the new baby."

"For us?" Mom said. She shook her head. "Don't be silly, Peter. You've been doing it for yourself."

"Don't bother us now," Dad said.

"But you have to watch it!" I said, my voice rising, the panic now growing in my chest and arms and legs. I remembered it from the last three times, the feeling that there was no way to get through to them, that I couldn't stand to be there anymore, beating my head against the cement wall of their coldness—that I had to get out of there and run. Was I going to dash into the street before the show even started?

But this time I thought first. And I knew what would work. "But I just have this *feeling*," I said. "Like when I knew to take care of Mom, and about the fire, and the car. This strong feeling that it's real important for all of us in this family for you to watch the show."

They looked at each other.

"But—" They both started to protest. But they couldn't. My "feelings" had been right three times before.

"Bring your knitting, Mom," I said. "Then it won't be a complete waste of time."

"Maybe we better go see what he's up to," Dad said. "Will it be over before the game starts?"

"Sure. Plenty of time."

They were looking at me and didn't see that a special news announcement was about to break into the TV show. It would be Meyer telling everybody it was really me who could see the future. I quickly switched off the TV.

They started down to the basement. I made sure the front door was locked and took the phone off the hook. How soon would the invasion start?

The stage was bigger and higher now, so they didn't have to look down at it. The lighting was better, too, not just the gooseneck lamp, but also a filtered spotlight on a tripod I had borrowed from the school, which sat well behind and above the two chairs and lit the red proscenium curtain with a dim and magical glow.

Mom and Dad sat down in silence.

I hurried backstage and up onto the bridge. I checked the location of all four puppets. I concentrated for a moment. Then I put my hand on the curtain.

"Ta-da!" I said, and pulled it open.

<<sixteen

<<**The backdrop was** sketchy—a barn with a silo on stage right, a farmhouse stage left, and in between them some chickens and cows and a plowed field in the background. The barn and the house were both open—you could see the outlines of them and also the insides. When the puppets were right in front of them, they were inside; and when they were in between them, they were outside.

There was an artist's easel drawn inside the barn.

The owner of the farm was working outside, in a sunbonnet and a checked dress with an apron. I got the fabric from scraps of material left over from a dress Mom made for herself last year. I had also tried to make her look like Mom, with blue eyes and high cheekbones.

"I love running a farm—but it's all work and no play," she said. "I wish there were more hours in the day."

I had my elbows on the bridge railing, working the controls with both hands. Sweat ran down my temples.

The puppet stood up straight, trembling a little because of my shaking, and put one hand over her eyes. "Who's that funny-looking person coming down the road?" I hitched her control to one of the many hooks above the stage, so that she could still be standing there while I worked the next puppet with both hands.

The boy puppet entered from the left. A drop of sweat fell onto the stage.

"What a funny-looking boy," the woman said again, to herself. "Long skinny neck and dark around the eyes."

I listened hard after this line. I could hear no reaction from Mom or Dad.

"Good afternoon, ma'am," I said in my own voice. "Nice day." I pulled the string at the base of the boy's spine, and he bowed to her. He held a suitcase, attached to him by a little metal hook in the palm of his hand.

"It's a nice day if you don't waste your time," the woman said.

"I'm looking for work," the boy said. "I got no home, no family. I can work hard—and help out in ways you wouldn't expect."

I took one hand off the boy puppet and used it to turn the woman's head to the side to make it look as if she was talking to herself. "Huh. Funny-looking kid. But I could use some help around here." I turned her head back to him. "Let's see how hard you can work. If you prove yourself, you can live here—room and board and maybe a home."

"Thank you, ma'am. You are very kind."

"You can sleep in the barn," she said. "The hay is soft, and some of it's even clean."

The boy put down his bag inside the barn, and I lifted its string and detached it from the hook on his hand. He went outside and worked—I hung him on a hook and moved his arms with one hand. Soon I turned off the gooseneck lamp. Night: The stage was dimmer in just the spotlight.

"Opening up my bag and taking out my easel," the boy said inside the barn. He had to say it, because the bag didn't really open, it just turned around and was white on the back. He hung it on a hook directly above the drawing of the easel on the backdrop. He stood in front of it and moved his hand up and down and around. "Painting—that's how I find out what's going to happen," he said.

I paused for a moment. In the quiet, I could hear Mom's knitting needles clicking—they sounded frantic.

"I can feel it now, what's going to happen," the boy said. He looked closer at the easel. "Cows getting sick."

Morning: "Hoof-and-mouth disease coming, ma'am. Keep your cows locked up, and they won't get sick."

"Nobody else said anything to me about it. But I'll listen to you just this once."

I quickly dropped down a piece of paper with "ONE WEEK LATER" written on it, then pulled it up again.

"Well, lucky for me I hired you, boy," the woman said. "Everybody around here has sick cows except me." She bent toward him. "How'd you know that was gonna happen, anyway?"

"Sometimes . . . I just know things," the boy said.

In the silence that followed, I noticed that Mom's needles weren't clicking. Was that a good sign or not?

Night: The boy painting. He looked closer at the easel. "The famous baseball star, coming nearby tomorrow."

The next morning, the boy was working outside, attached to a hook, when the baseball star came striding along. He looked like Dad—curly brown hair, prominent nose. I worked the controls slowly so that his movement was very strong and emphatic. It helped that his feet were weighted.

"Hello!" the boy called out to him. "Aren't you the famous baseball star Mr. Frank?"

"That's right, son," he said in a very deep, manly voice. He went over next to the boy and lifted his hand to gesture at the scene. "Beautiful farm here. Never would have seen it if it weren't for you calling out to me."

"The woman who owns it is very kind—and pretty, too."

The boy and the man were both attached to hooks so I could use two hands to bring the woman walking gracefully over to them—my hands were not shaking as much; I was gaining control.

Then I remembered the sensation of the car hitting me, and my hands started shaking again. I felt as if I was going to throw up or faint, as if I had to sit down and couldn't go on with the show. And how soon were all the people from Meyer's house going to show up?

I gulped and kept on going. "What are you doing around here?" the woman asked the ballplayer.

"I love farm country. I always wanted to live on a farm when I stop playing. Can I look around?"

I dropped the "ONE WEEK LATER" sign again.

"What're you doing back here?" the woman asked the baseball star.

"Couldn't keep away, ma'am. And not just because of the farm. I had to see you again."

"Don't waste my time with sweet talk."

"Don't know *how* to sweet talk. Only know how I feel

about you. I'm tired of baseball—my playing days are over. And now I've found what I want in life—thanks to that funny-looking boy who works for you."

I lowered another sign. It had ribbons and flowers on it, and bells ringing, and it said, "WEDDING BELLS."

While the sign was down, I had a chance to look at my watch. Ten minutes to eight. The panic got worse. Could I finish it in time? Would I be dead in fifteen minutes?

Night: The boy painting in the barn. "Frank and Gert are so happy together," he said. He bent over the painting. "What's this? A new addition! But don't want to spring this on them fast—just make sure she's careful."

Morning: All three working. "Better take it easy, ma'am," the boy said. "We can do the heavy work."

"Who's giving the orders around here?" the woman said.

The man said in his deep voice, "Maybe he's right. Don't want you tiring yourself out when you don't need to."

"Well, if you say so, Frank." She went inside.

"It was you who brought me here," the man said to the boy. "And Gert told me you knew about the hoof-and-mouth disease. Now you're telling her to take it easy. Why?"

"Just trying to do what I can to help."

I took a deep breath, feeling my gut tightening. Did I really dare to say the next line? But I had planned it carefully. I couldn't back down now. I wouldn't have been able to say it if I hadn't been hidden by the big piece of red-and-gold cloth.

"Both so good to me," the boy said. "Giving me a home and a job. Never a harsh word to me, even though I'm so funny-looking. So I just want to help you in return."

"Why be harsh when we know you mean so well?" the man said in his deep, resonant voice.

I quickly switched off the light.

The boy painting in the barn. He made a joyful jump. "I'm so happy! All three of them will be fine."

And I was wondering if I would live to see the baby.

Morning: The boy went over to his hook, where he always stood while doing farmwork.

Now came the most difficult moment in the show. I tried not to think about how I had tangled and dropped the alien puppet the other time, when what I was doing then was so much easier than this. I tried not to think about the feeling of the car hitting me. I prayed the people from Meyer's house would stay away for another minute or two.

I held the woman and the baby puppet made by Meyer in one hand, the man in the other. With the baby resting in her arms, the woman stepped onstage, the man beside her. I had to get them over to their hooks, gracefully, neatly, without mishap. Three puppets at once.

The baby control slid in my slippery grasp as I tilted my hand to make the woman walk. With my left hand, which was holding the man, I pushed the baby control back up onto my right fingers. The man lurched a little, bumping into the woman. But I got them safely attached to their hooks, the baby closely cradled in the mother's arms.

I wanted to see what kind of a picture the mother, father, and baby made, standing there together. I hoped the effect was like a real piece of sculpture that could move.

"A beautiful baby!" the boy cried. "Such a happy moment. But a sad one for me. Because now I have to go."

"Go? Why are you going?" the woman said.

"I've been happy with you. But my time here is over; my job is done. I can't see what's going to happen in the future here anymore. That's finished. Now you have a prosperous farm and a family and everything you want. I have to move on. That's my life."

The family was safely in place, so I could use both my hands to make the boy pick up his easel bag and hook it onto his hand. "Thank you so much and good luck always," he said, and walked off the stage.

"He helped us so much," the man said. "Who—or what—was he?"

"We will never know," the mother said. I moved her head to make her look down at the baby. "Time for your breakfast, baby," she said, and walked offstage.

The man stood looking after the boy.

I glanced at my watch. It was exactly eight o'clock.

I pulled the curtain shut and unplugged the spotlight.

There was no sound from the audience.

<<seventeen

<<still silence, and no sign of movement.

I couldn't just go on hiding behind the red-and-gold cloth. I stepped out in front of the stage. "It's after eight o'clock," I said. "The game started."

Mom and Dad both were still sitting there. They weren't meeting my eye, or each other's; they didn't know where to look.

But they weren't racing upstairs to watch the game.

"I finished just in time," I pointed out. "If you miss the game, it's not my fault."

"What was he supposed to be, the puppet that looked like you?" Dad asked me. "Some kind of angel or something? Is that how you see yourself?"

It could have been an accusation—except he didn't sound angry. "I don't know what he was. It was just a story," I said, and cleared my throat. "Sometimes you can't explain stories. They just kind of tell themselves."

"What kind of excuse is that?" he asked me. "You're the one who made up the story."

"And your father, a baseball star," Mom said. Could there possibly be a hint of a smile on her lips? I hardly dared to believe it.

"What's wrong with that?" Dad asked her. "You think it's funny or something, me being a baseball star?"

"No, Frank, that's not what I mean." She lifted her needles, then set them back in her lap again. She pressed her lips together and still wouldn't meet my eye. I had rarely seen her so unsure of herself. "Well, I don't know, Peter. . . ." She paused and took a deep breath. "Well, maybe it wasn't such a waste of time after all," she admitted. "As long as you do better in math and start playing outside more, now that you did it."

"But if the kid who looked like you wasn't an angel, then why did he leave at the end?" Dad asked me. He was always quicker to say what was on his mind than Mom was. "You don't think we want you to leave, because of the new baby, do you?"

Mom's eyes widened. "Frank, don't you say such a thing!" she said angrily. She turned to me, suddenly shy.

"You're our son, Peter, and this is your home. It always will be."

"Now . . . I know that," I said.

And finally I let the relief flow through me. My body felt like water; I wanted to sink to the floor. Mom and Dad had never said anything like that before.

I'm not going to die. I'm not going to die. I'm not going to die, I was silently rejoicing.

"That puppet that looked like you, he knew what was going to happen," Dad said. "And so did you. Was it from *painting* that you knew?"

Maybe I wasn't home free yet. I shrugged. "Oh, you mean those feelings I had about the future. They're gone now. That will never happen again. So don't expect it."

"What's that supposed to mean?" Dad said.

"I just don't think I'll have those feelings anymore, that's all." I shrugged.

"Well, maybe this puppet stuff wasn't so sissy after all," Dad said, and stood up. But oddly, he didn't head for the stairs and the TV. "Lemme see how you did all that. I don't see how one kid could work all those puppets at the same time, without any mistakes. What have you got back there now anyway?" And he walked behind the stage.

I heard the needles clicking as Mom began knitting again—staying down in the basement, too.

"Wait right here. I'll be back in half a second," I said.

Much as I hated to risk ruining this moment, I had to see what had happened with Meyer.

Upstairs I hung up the phone, then picked it up again when the dial tone came back and called Eloise.

"What happened?" she said. "Did you do it yet?"

"Yes! And everything's fine. I did something right for a change."

"I'm so happy, Peter." She sounded like she was crying.

"What about that special news flash? We missed it. Was it Meyer? Nobody's bugging me yet."

"It was about Meyer. But he didn't give you away— he said he pretended he could see the future because his friend who really could do it wanted to be anonymous. No names. Now his family's going out of town until this blows over." She paused. "He did something right, too."

I said good-bye and hung up, feeling relieved all over again.

I didn't know what was going to happen next, just the way it had been so long ago when I was living my original life for the first time. No predicting anymore. From now on, every moment would be a step into the unknown.

And yet, I had never felt so sure of myself. I had set out to do something that had seemed almost impossible, and I had succeeded. I had never done that before.

And I wondered: Why had I been given three chances?

Could it possibly be because I was intended to paint or build or design something really important? Something that might change the world?

I probably wouldn't know the answer to that for a long, long time. But for now—I hurried down to join Mom and Dad in the basement.